Ian Rankin

The International Number One Bestseller

'Unsurpassed among living British crime writers'
The Times

'Worthy of Agatha Christie at her best'   *Scotsman*

'Britain's best crime novelist'   *Express*

'Rankin is a master storyteller'   *Guardian*

'One of Britain's leading novelists in any genre'
New Statesman

'Britain's finest detective novelist'   *Scotland on Sunday*

Rona Munro

Giles Cooper Award, Susan Smith Blackburn Prize, Evening Standard Award, Writers' Guild of Great Britain Award

'A powerful storyteller immersed in the nuances of human relationships'   *Observer*

'Rona Munro's triptych of historical dramas both informs and transcends Scotland's independence debate'
Financial Times on *The James Plays*

'Powerfully involving'   *Independent* on *Iron*

'Unnervingly good British drama' *New York Times* on *Iron*

'Rona Munro's thrilling trilogy could be the finest history plays ever penned'   *Telegraph* on *The James Plays*

Also by Ian Rankin

The Detective Malcolm Fox Series

The Complaints

The Impossible Dead

The Detective Inspector Rebus Series

Knots & Crosses

Hide & Seek

Tooth & Nail
(previously published as Wolfman*)*

Strip Jack

The Black Book

Mortal Causes

Let it Bleed

Black & Blue

The Hanging Garden

Death is Not the End
(a novella)

Dead Souls

Set in Darkness

The Falls

Resurrection Men

A Question of Blood

Fleshmarket Close

The Naming of the Dead

Exit Music

Standing in
Another Man's Grave

Saints of the Shadow Bible

Even Dogs in the Wild

Rather Be the Devil

Other Novels

The Flood

Watchman

Westwind

Doors Open

Writing as Jack Harvey

Witch Hunt

Bleeding Hearts

Blood Hunt

Short Stories

A Good Hanging and
Other Stories

Beggars Banquet

The Beat Goes On

Plays

Dark Road

All Ian Rankin's titles are available on audio.
Also available: *Jackie Leven Said* by Ian Rankin and Jackie
Leven.

IAN RANKIN
& RONA MUNRO
REBUS:
LONG SHADOWS

THE REHEARSAL SCRIPT

ORION

First published in Great Britain in 2018 by Orion Books
an imprint of The Orion Publishing Group Ltd
Carmelite House, 50 Victoria Embankment
London EC4Y 0DZ

An Hachette UK Company

1 3 5 7 9 10 8 6 4 2

Rebus: Long Shadows was first performed at The
Birmingham Repertory Theatre on 20th September 2018.
Produced by Daniel Schumann, Lee Dean and Cambridge
Arts Theatre in association with Birmingham Repertory
Theatre.

A CIP catalogue record for this book is
available from the British Library.

ISBN (Hardback) 978 1 4091 8574 1
ISBN (eBook) 978 1 4091 8576 5

Printed in Great Britain by Clays Ltd, Elcograf S.p.A.

MIX
Paper from
responsible sources
FSC
www.fsc.org
FSC® C104740

www.orionbooks.co.uk

Ian Rankin is the multi-million copy worldwide bestseller of over thirty novels and creator of John Rebus. His books have been translated into thirty-six languages and have been adapted for radio, the stage and the screen.

Rankin is the recipient of four Crime Writers' Association Dagger Awards, including the Diamond Dagger, the UK's most prestigious award for crime fiction. In the United States, he has won the celebrated Edgar Award and been shortlisted for the Anthony Award. In Europe, he has won Denmark's Palle Rosenkrantz Prize, the French Grand Prix du Roman Noir and the German Deutscher Krimipreis.

He is the recipient of honorary degrees from universities across the UK, is a Fellow of The Royal Society of Edinburgh and a Fellow of The Royal Society of Literature, and has received an OBE for his services to literature.

Website: IanRankin.net
Twitter: @Beathhigh
Facebook: IanRankinBooks

Rona Munro has written extensively for stage, radio, film and television. Her theatre credits include *Lucy Barton* – a one-woman show performed by Laura Linney at The Bridge Theatre London in 2018; *The James Plays* – a trilogy of award-winning plays produced by the National Theatre of Scotland, The National Theatre UK and Edinburgh International Festival; *Scuttlers*; *Little Eagles* and *Iron*, for which she won the John Whiting Award in 2003. Her television credits include the BAFTA-nominated *Bumping the Odds*, and her films include the Ken Loach film *Ladybird Ladybird*, and *Oranges and Sunshine*, directed by Jim Loach. Her work for radio includes several dramas for The Stanley Baxter Playhouse. Rona is the only writer so far to have contributed episodes to both the 'classic' and contemporary series of *Doctor Who*.

REBUS:
LONG SHADOWS

THE REHEARSAL SCRIPT

INTRODUCTION

It was theatre producer Daniel Schumann who first mooted to me the idea of putting John Rebus on the stage. I'd be lying, however, if I said the notion hadn't crossed my mind from time to time. I've never been in the same room with Rebus, you see, never watched him in three dimensions as he wrestles with a problem or wrangles with his (considerable) demons. I had co-written one stage play in the recent past, *Dark Road*, working alongside the Lyceum Theatre's artistic director Mark Thomson, who also happens to be a hugely talented playwright. That play was a psychodrama set in contemporary Edinburgh and featuring a senior police officer at the end of her career, looking back on the one case from her early years that had never been resolved to her satisfaction while also coping with her demanding teenage daughter.

The challenge there had been, in part, to satisfy audiences that they weren't just watching Rebus with a sex change. Indeed, with the benefit of hindsight, I think I was anxious not to pen a drama about a character who had been such a large part of my writing life. I wanted to break from Rebus, to write an original story rather than an adaptation.

I'm still not one for adaptation.

Early on, as Daniel and I discussed the project, we decided that this would hopefully be an all-new story, set at a slight remove from the universe of the Rebus novels. Rona Munro's name cropped up very early in our conversations as someone who might work in partnership to bring Rebus to the stage, and to life. I'd been a fan of Rona's writing for many years, not least her vast undertaking for the National Theatre of Scotland, *The James Plays*. I was really keen for her 'take' on Rebus. At our first meeting, she stressed that the story ahead of us would have to be one that could only be told by means of a stage play. We wanted something that would satisfy fans of the books, but also work on its own merits for theatregoers not acquainted with the characters.

We met for long brain-storming sessions in my living-room, fuelled by hot drinks and the occasional lunch at a nearby bistro. We talked about Rebus, about what sort of man he was and how he had become that man. We analysed Cafferty and Cafferty's relationship with Rebus. And Rebus's relationship with Detective Inspector Siobhan Clarke. We also touched on the city which surrounded all three, Edinburgh, a city with its own secrets and foibles and ghosts. Rebus, of course, has always been a haunted man – haunted by victims, by unsolved cases, by his inability to deal satisfactorily with his nemesis Cafferty. But haunted, too, by his own self-perceived failings as husband, father and friend.

The play we were feeling our way towards – *Long Shadows* – would be a character study, a whodunit, and a piece of choreography in which the central trio dance around each other as allegiances shift and hidden truths eventually reach the spotlight.

Talking, of course, is one thing, creating quite another.

Having workshopped ideas and even storyboarded the arc, much of the hard work then fell to Rona. She knows only too well what works and doesn't work on a stage. As a novelist, I can shovel into a book all the pages, scene-changes and characters I need. This is impossible to replicate on the stage. Rona had to take my story and make it work within a very tight framework. Drafts began to bounce between us, as difficulties emerged and were dealt with, problems and niggles ironed out. But the real heart of the play didn't change much. There stood Rebus and Cafferty, two men of advanced years whose world is no longer what it was. Faced by change and decay in all they see, their empathy is matched only by their antipathy. They understand one another – might even actually respect certain aspects of one another – and yet each would gladly take the other down. Indeed, no other ending would seem satisfactory.

This was another decision that we took early on: the play would feature the 'older' Rebus, the one readers of today have got to know. I began the series when I was twenty-five and Rebus was forty. He is now in his mid-sixties, retired, and yet unable to slough off the skin of the detective he once and for so long was. He has an itch, too, represented by Cafferty – the one who got away.

Cafferty stands for every villain Rebus has encountered, every act of unfeeling cruelty fuelled by greed and anger. While Rebus seethes quietly in his tenement flat, music and alcohol keeping him company, Cafferty keeps watch over the city from his penthouse eyrie, fearful that all he has gained can still be snatched from him if he makes one single mistake.

All of this will be familiar to readers of the novels, but incidents and characters occur in *Long Shadows* which won't be found in the books. We have played with elements of Rebus's history – and Cafferty's – to make for an engrossing two hours of theatre, even if it means stepping out of the universe of the books into a parallel world that is *almost* identical. I agreed wholeheartedly with Rona that the play had to work within its own system and on its own merits. Over the course of our collaboration she dug deep into the characters' psyches and motivations, making me consider difficult questions and bringing me to a more rounded understanding of the interior lives of Rebus, Cafferty and Siobhan Clarke. I have said in the past that I keep writing about Rebus because I haven't got to the heart of what makes him tick. Working with Rona took me closer than ever before.

One thing I know from my previous play, however, is that the writing is only one part of the whole. As I pen these words, rehearsals have yet to start. The main casting has been done, but minor roles remain to be filled. I have not seen the stage design or the costumes, nor heard the actors speak the lines. In rehearsal, the lines begin to lift from the page and take flight, becoming closer to music than to ink. They flit around the actors until the actors begin to fade and become the characters themselves. It's a magical process. And when rehearsals are done and the action shifts to the stage, scenery completed, lighting devised, music ready . . . Well, that's when *Long Shadows* truly becomes a thing in itself, independent of the authors who were there at its conception.

Rebus has cast a long shadow in the thirty years since he sprang to life between the pages of that first adventure, *Knots and Crosses*. He seems, however, more fully alive to me with each passing year and in each new episode of his career. He is complex, stubborn, intelligent, driven, and hard-edged. And in *Long Shadows* he needs to be at his sharpest, because forces are massing against him and both past and present are about to deal him blows heavier than any he has previously experienced. In Edinburgh, that most spectral of cities, Rebus knows the dead don't always rest quietly, while the living remain troubled and – just occasionally – deadly dangerous.

Welcome to the world of Rebus. Welcome to *Long Shadows* . . .

Ian Rankin

CHARACTERS

John Rebus Retired detective

Heather Ross Daughter of unsolved murder victim
  Maggie Towler

Andy Neighbour to John Rebus

Maggie Towler Heather Ross's mother

Siobhan Clarke Detective Inspector

Angela Simpson Cold case murder victim

Barman A barman

Charlie Informant

Big Ger Cafferty Crime boss of Edinburgh, long-term
  nemesis to John Rebus

Mordaunt Suspected murderer of Angela Simpson

Detective A police detective

Technician A police technician

Act One

The stairwell at Arden Street

HEATHER, a very young woman, is slumped on the stair.
She's dressed for a night out, revealing but not startling
clothes, typical Saturday night girl out clubbing with mates.
She's plugged into her music. Now she sings along, a few
lines, pure and accapella. The track she hears is audible
only to her. She stops singing, moving gently to the song.
She's mellow and relaxed with something but not obviously
under the influence. REBUS is coming up the stairs. He sees
HEATHER. He checks for a moment. Looking at her.

REBUS   Comfy there are you?

HEATHER doesn't seem to have heard him, lost in her music.
He carries on past her. HEATHER sings again, just the one
line, pure and beautiful. REBUS stops dead. He walks slowly
back down to HEATHER.

REBUS   You're too young to know that one.

She can't hear him, he mimes for her to pull out her
earphones. She does.

REBUS   You're too young to know that one.

HEATHER   *(Frampton Comes Alive, 'Show Me the*
               Way') 1976. It's my family heirloom.

REBUS   How's that?

3

HEATHER	My Mum loved it. It was her favourite song when she was a tiny tiny wee girl.
REBUS	Is that right? I know you don't I? I know your face.
HEATHER	Don't think so.
REBUS	Waiting for someone?
HEATHER	I was just having a wee think.
REBUS	Who're you after? Which flat?
HEATHER	He's no in. I'm freezing. Can I wait in yours?
REBUS	No.
HEATHER	How no?
REBUS	Because you shouldny be sitting about on the stairs at 2 a.m. dressed like that and you definitely shouldny be asking to get into strange men's flats.
HEATHER	Who are you? My Grandad?
REBUS	Apparently I could be.
HEATHER	So . . . what? You're a murdering rapist that'll cut me up with a steak knife?
REBUS	Well I could be that too. How do you know?
HEATHER	Are you?
REBUS	No . . . but . . .

HEATHER   So what do you do then?

REBUS   I was a policeman. Which makes me a bit of an expert on the kind of trouble wee lassies can get into on a Friday night.

HEATHER   A policeman? Wow. Aye, now you say it I can see it. You, have got the shiniest shoes I've ever, ever seen.

REBUS   Ah, that's an army habit. I was in the paras once . . .

HEATHER   Seriously? So did you like kill people with floss tape? Gouge out their eyes with your thumbs?

REBUS   No. I'll get you a cab home.

HEATHER   I'm staying here.

REBUS   Not an option.

HEATHER   Aye come on, I've got police protection.

REBUS   I'm retired. And I never did waste time protecting folk from their own stupidity.

HEATHER   You think I don't know the worst that could happen?

REBUS   I think you imagine it'll never happen to you.

HEATHER   It happened to my Mum. Strangled and dumped on a building site beside the

Jackdaw pub in Newhaven. So there you go. I do know.

REBUS   When?

HEATHER   2001. I don't remember her, I was a baby. Gran brought me up. Mum got killed 'cause she went out on the raz. A good Mummy wouldny be out with a wee bairn at hame eh? She was always falling into trouble, first me, then death . . . She was just my age. Can you imagine it? I'm no getting lumbered with a bairn till I've made my money. Money first. Then we'll see about getting domestic.

REBUS has placed the memory.

REBUS   Maggie Towler.

HEATHER   Aye! Jeez you really are polis eh? Aw Christ . . . was it . . . did you . . .?

REBUS   No, I wasn't lead on that case. Remember it though.

HEATHER   That's nice. That she's remembered. When I play that song I tell myself I'm talking to her. It's about the only thing I've got that's hers.

REBUS   I thought you looked familiar. That must be why. Maggie Towler's daughter.

HEATHER	You remember her face?
REBUS	I remember all the faces. And most of the names. What's your name?
HEATHER	Heather. Heather Ross.
REBUS	Not Towler?
HEATHER	I got Gran's name. What's yours?
REBUS	John Rebus. So what about your Dad?
HEATHER	I don't know. Gran said she didny know either but that was lies. She didny want me thinking about him. 'Your mother thought she could take on the world. Then she met a man she couldny handle.'
REBUS	Every Granny's warning.
HEATHER	Can you do me a favour John?
REBUS	I try to avoid them. Go on, what?
HEATHER	You've still got all my Mum's stuff. The police have, I mean. Her clothes, the jewellery she was wearing . . .
REBUS	It's evidence.
HEATHER	How can it be evidence when she's been dead seventeen years?
REBUS	It's an unsolved murder. So we . . . *(corrects himself)* . . . they, try and keep the evidence. Forensics get better all the time. DNA

testing gets better all the time. One day we might be able to nail the bastard.

HEATHER   You're still trying to catch him?

REBUS   Never close an unsolved killing.

HEATHER   What if he's dead? The guy that did it to her?

REBUS   Then he got away with murder.

HEATHER   That'd shred me. I'd rather never know than that . . .

REBUS   Where do you need to get back to Heather?

HEATHER   What?

REBUS   Where do you live?

HEATHER   Och around and about.

REBUS   Where does Gran live?

HEATHER   You ask a lot of questions eh?

REBUS   Canny seem to break the habit.

HEATHER   My Gran's dead. Home was Newhaven, the scuzzy bit that's still scuzzy.

REBUS   The Jackdaw pub.

HEATHER   Aye, that's still there. It's a club now. Techno grunge every Friday. They get artists in from all over. Have you been?

REBUS   What do you think?

HEATHER   You canny dance to it?

REBUS   Canny dance to anything. Wouldn't try.

HEATHER   I love dancing. You think that's creepy? That I go the pub she did? The pub where she had her last drink.

REBUS   No. No I can understand why you might do that.

HEATHER   Don't always think about her. She went out drinking and took the short cut home through the building site. Sometimes I get really mad at her for being that stupid. I knew better before I was ten. So you'll help me?

REBUS   What?

HEATHER   You'll see if they're still trying to catch the guy that killed her? Chase up your pals in the police?

REBUS   I haven't got many pals in the police. Never did.

HEATHER   But you could phone somebody.

REBUS   No. Look, I know it's hard but you'd best forget it. Live your life. You don't always get an answer.

HEATHER   I bet you could always get an answer.

REBUS   If I could, I'd sleep better.

HEATHER   Do you have nightmares then?

REBUS   Only since I stopped drinking.

HEATHER   Christ that'll dae it.

A young man ANDY is coming up the stairs. He stops dead when he sees HEATHER and REBUS.

HEATHER   You're late. I nearly called the polis on you.

ANDY   *(wary)* You been talking to him?

REBUS   Any reason she shouldn't?

HEATHER   *(on the move)* Come on then . . . What's your name again?

ANDY says nothing.

REBUS   A. Lamont. That's what it says on the bit of cardboard. Don't know what the A stands for. Archibald?

ANDY   Andy.

REBUS   Just being neighbourly Andy. *(to Heather)* You should maybe ask him how he's supplementing his income. Doesny look like an impoverished student to me.

HEATHER   No?

REBUS   His post says he's a student. Mature student is it Andy? Second degree? Don't get your fees paid for that do you? How do you manage? Are you doing a wee sideline in pharmaceuticals? If I've noticed . . . *(let's that one hang)*

ANDY   Fuck off.

HEATHER   You've noticed him dealing?

REBUS   Are you surprised? Isn't that why you're here?

HEATHER   No. No it's not.

REBUS   Glad to hear it.

ANDY is still warily watching REBUS as HEATHER makes her way back upstairs.

HEATHER   I'm just visiting. I'm going to ask you again John. I think you're the man that can help me.

REBUS   I don't change my mind.

HEATHER   No? Don't say things like that. I love a challenge. See you John.

She's gone. REBUS is still watching ANDY.

ANDY   What do you think you're looking at?

REBUS   I'll let you know.

> *REBUS waits until ANDY goes upstairs. REBUS tries to get in, doesn't have key. He searches all his pockets. It's not there. Swears. Takes one from top of door jamb. Goes into his own flat—*

Rebus's Arden Street flat/dream

He's walked into darkness. A young woman, MAGGIE, stands on her own, the only thing lit in darkness. She's played by the same actress who plays HEATHER but MAGGIE is dressed differently, a coat from 2001 fashion, a scarf round her neck. She's dancing to the same song, half singing along. We can't see her face clearly.

REBUS   What are you doing here?

MAGGIE   Sit down John.

REBUS sits down in an armchair and watches as if this is television.

REBUS   Who are you?

MAGGIE   I thought you never forgot a face, or a name. You let me down John Rebus . . .

Rebus's Arden Street flat

Lights snap up as REBUS *wakes in his armchair. It was a dream. He's fallen asleep in the chair. The song is still playing, just the last line, stuck on repeat.* SIOBHAN *has walked in. She goes and lifts the needle off the record.*

SIOBHAN   So there's something you need to know about twenty-first-century etiquette. If you get a dozen texts and you don't answer inside twenty-four hours everyone thinks you're dead.

There's an empty glass beside REBUS'S *chair. He picks it up and stares at it.* SIOBHAN *takes it out of his hand and replaces it with a take-away coffee.*

SIOBHAN   And I thought you weren't doing this any more.

REBUS   Doing what?

SIOBHAN   Drinking yourself to sleep in an armchair.

REBUS   Did I do that?

SIOBHAN   Pretty conclusive evidence.

REBUS   'Time is it?

SIOBHAN   Time to check your phone.

REBUS mutters swearing as he pushes out of the chair and leaves the room, going to the bathroom.

SIOBHAN   *(calling after him)* Don't mind me. I'll just make myself at home.

She makes a half-hearted attempt to clear a few things up. Quickly gives up.

SIOBHAN   I'd make you another cup of coffee but I'm betting you've no milk.

She finds his phone. Sighs. REBUS comes back into the room, towelling his face. She holds up the phone at him. Accusing.

SIOBHAN   And you've no juice. Where's your charger?

She's looking for it, finding it, plugging in his phone.

REBUS   I do have a landline. You've heard of them? Ancient communication devices, never run out of juice?

SIOBHAN   I rang it. About half one?

REBUS   I was out.

SIOBHAN   Doing what?

REBUS   Walking.

SIOBHAN   Wandering round the Meadows in the
            middle of the night.

REBUS   Wandering's part of my ongoing exercise
            regime.

She's got the whisky bottle.

SIOBHAN   Is this part of your exercise regime?

REBUS   Better than sleeping pills. Natural product.
            Organic.

SIOBHAN   That's great. You can put it on your muesli
            instead of milk.

REBUS   Muesli? I forgot my keys last night. Ageing
            brain. Too much content, no enough storage.

SIOBHAN   Throw some of the memories away.

REBUS   Working on it.

*There are boxes and stacks of files all over the floor. REBUS
is starting to look through these as they talk.*

SIOBHAN   Don't you want to know why I was trying to
            get hold of you?

REBUS   Aren't you here to tell me?

SIOBHAN   No, I came round looking for proof of life.

REBUS   But since you're here . . .?

SIOBHAN   They're going to offer it.

REBUS   Promotion?

SIOBHAN   Had one of those 'strictly between us but
         you might want to buy some smarter suits'
         conversations.

REBUS   Well that's great! *(she's not responding)* Isn't
         it great?

SIOBHAN   Just wanted to talk to you.

REBUS   What's to talk about? About time isn't it?

SIOBHAN   So I'd be crazy to knock it back?

REBUS   You want to be stalled at detective inspector
         for the rest of your days?

SIOBHAN   I could do something else.

REBUS   You're no fit to do anything else.

SIOBHAN   Hey. We're not all as sad as you! Some of us
         have other things in their lives apart from
         the job.

REBUS   Like what? Driving to Hibs away games?
         That's a fast track to suicidal depression.

   *REBUS is still half looking for something in his heaps of
   paper.*

SIOBHAN   I could do another job!

REBUS   No you couldn't.

SIOBHAN   Well thanks for the vote of confidence. What
             are you doing?

REBUS   I just remembered something, about an old
             case.

SIOBHAN   What old case?

REBUS   A murder, 2001.

SIOBHAN   Seriously?

REBUS   Aye, I passed on it when it came in. Maggie
             Towler? Remember?

SIOBHAN   No.

REBUS   No, well, we were a bit busy that year. I bet
             you remember that.

SIOBHAN   Only on the bad nights. We've had worse
             years since.

REBUS   I was starting that case with you. I pushed
             Maggie Towler onto Fraser Morris. *(he's
             found the file he wants)* Got it! *(looking through
             file)* Fraser was a sloppy wee shite, I think
             he just read the notes of the first officer on
             the scene and filed it as a lost cause.

SIOBHAN   So I want career advice and you want to
             rerun some whinge from 2001? Are you
             even listening?

REBUS   Take the promotion. You've come too far to
        stop now.

SIOBHAN Have I?

REBUS   It's our anniversary.

SIOBHAN What?

REBUS   Twenty-five years since I started mentoring
        your illustrious career.

SIOBHAN Oh is that what you were doing?

REBUS   Helping you scale the heights of Police
        Scotland, Shiv.

SIOBHAN Keeping me on the brink of investigation
        for professional misconduct.

REBUS   The edge that sharpens the detective
        senses.

SIOBHAN Is it really twenty-five years?

REBUS   I counted.

SIOBHAN You're right. It must be. Because I arrived
        just after the first time we tried to convict
        Mordaunt.

REBUS   Is that what's got you in this state? The
        Mordaunt case?

SIOBHAN I'm not in a state. Alright. I want the right
        result this time. I want that a *lot*. But you

must be feeling that. You were part of the
original investigation . . .

REBUS   I was just a baby detective. All I did was
               a wee bit of the leg work. But everyone
               was part of it . . . Something about it, it
               got to everyone. You know that last lassie
               he killed . . . Angela . . . *(trying to get name)*
               Jesus . . . dying brain . . .

SIOBHAN   *(cutting in)* Angela Simpson.

REBUS   Aye. That was her first proper night out
               you know. First time her Mum and Dad let
               her stay out past eleven. A sixteen year old
               lassie just excited to be out on a Saturday
               . . . Is it the Dad you're getting ready for
               court?

SIOBHAN   Yes.

REBUS   How's he doing?

SIOBHAN   He's still blaming himself: 'If I'd known she
               was going drinking . . .' Sixteen. You ought
               to be able to sneak into a pub kidding on
               you're old enough, laughing with all your
               mates. That shouldn't get you killed.

REBUS   Sixteen. Still new. Still daft enough to fall for
               it when some older guy starts chatting you
               up. Young enough to swallow the lines . . .

SIOBHAN   But Jesus, look at Mordaunt!

REBUS   Aye. Even when he was young he looked like a feral weasel that lived in a sewer. He must have had some chat up lines.

SIOBHAN   He'd've had confidence by the time he murdered Angela wouldn't he? He'd already got away with rape and murder twice.

REBUS   He was a cocky swaggering little prick. Then and now.

SIOBHAN   Now we'll get him. The forensics will get him.

REBUS   Is it from the tights? Is the evidence on the tights he strangled them with?

SIOBHAN   Come on John, I'm not supposed to talk about ongoing . . .

REBUS   (cutting in) Aw come on yourself, that's no even me guessing. He strangled those girls with their own tights. There must be traces the forensics weren't good enough to catch at the time, but you can prove the bastard's hands were on the knots now.

SIOBHAN   Alright. Good guess. Hopefully, finally, we can do a proper job of putting him away.

REBUS   You don't think we did a proper job back in 1992?

SIOBHAN   I'm not saying that . . .

REBUS   Sounds like you are.

SIOBHAN   Look, I can't help adding up the evidence
           the original detectives had. They had
           Mordaunt's plumbers' van parked up near
           where the young women vanished, three
           times. Every murder, there's his van . . .

REBUS   And there's his wife, giving him an alibi,
           every time.

SIOBHAN   And, ok, you find yourself thinking, 'How
           hard did they lean on his wife?' Because
           she must have known.

REBUS   Why would you want to know a thing like
           that? Way I heard it she was like concrete.
           They couldny budge her. Mordaunt was
           drinking with her, apparently, every time.

SIOBHAN   CCTV evidence might've knocked a hole in
           that lie now. Forensics would have nailed
           him, *will* nail him now . . . if nothing goes
           wrong.

REBUS   What might go wrong?

SIOBHAN   The trial starts Monday.

REBUS   I know. And what might go wrong? What're
           you worried about?

SIOBHAN   Nothing. Nothing at all. Do I look worried?

REBUS   Yes.

SIOBHAN   You see you think you can read me but this
           just proves . . .

REBUS   (cutting her off) Why haven't I been called to
           give evidence?

SIOBHAN   You just said it. You weren't doing more
           than door to door back then. You weren't
           the lead detective. Steve Cant was.

REBUS   Steve Cant couldny lead his own shite out
           his arse. It's thanks to him we never nailed
           the pervy weasel the day we lifted him. He
           was so busy worrying about playing it by
           the book he barely asked Mordaunt his
           name and address . . .

SIOBHAN   (cutting in) It's thanks to him and the
           forensic pathologist at the time that the
           evidence of the Angela's clothing has been
           preserved properly all these years. Stored
           properly, logged properly, and believe me
           that's going to be an issue for the defence.

       Something in her tone alerts REBUS.

REBUS   What's happened?

SIOBHAN   You did put Mordaunt away John. You got
           him the same year Angela died. For assault.

REBUS   Aye. What about it?

SIOBHAN   What made you so sure it was him?

REBUS   I could see rapist murdering scum beneath
             that cheery plumber exterior.

SIOBHAN   And could you really see the kind of man
             that could lay out a man twice his size? A
             man like Morris Gerald Cafferty?

REBUS   Cafferty was hit from behind.

SIOBHAN   True.

REBUS   And that was twenty-five years ago. Cafferty
             wasn't the behemoth of crime and chaos he
             was in his prime.

SIOBHAN   He was a big man. And a lethal one.

REBUS   He turned his back for two minutes. All it
             took.

SIOBHAN   But I never understood why he let
             Mordaunt get away with it.

REBUS   How do you mean?

SIOBHAN   Well . . . Mordaunt mugs him behind one of
             his own bars, length of wood to the back of
             the skull . . . What was the motive anyway?

REBUS   Said Cafferty owed him for a plumbing
             repair on his indoor pool. Cafferty said the
             job was shoddy.

SIOBHAN   So he whacked the most feared crime boss
             in Edinburgh . . .

REBUS   *(cutting in)* He wasny quite that then but . . .

SIOBHAN   *(cutting in)* And Cafferty lets him live?

REBUS   We put him away for it. That was one time Mordaunt's van in the car park was good enough evidence to convince a jury. Justice was done.

SIOBHAN   Since when does Big Ger Cafferty ever settle for our justice over his?

REBUS   And since when is it justice when a lying, murdering rapist gets away with only eighteen months for assault? Christ, it haunted everyone you know? Angela Simpson, just sixteen. In the photo in the incident room she was in her school uniform . . .

ANGELA walks through the scene, half dancing to music she's quietly humming or in her head, aware of nothing else. This is just in REBUS's mind's eye.

REBUS   At least we got him for something.

SIOBHAN   That was the attitude at the time? From you and your fellow officers?

REBUS   The gutters ran with IPA and single malt. The fatted calf was put in a bun. Songs of triumph were sung. Aye. It was a result. A bit of one. A crumb of comfort.

SIOBHAN   You see, I don't think that's going to help.

REBUS   Help what? *(she hesitates)* Siobhan? Tell me!

SIOBHAN   I heard the defence think they have something. Something to put up against the forensic evidence. We think they're going to suggest that someone tampered with the evidence that helped you put Mordaunt away for assaulting Big Ger.

REBUS   Why would we tamper with that evidence?

SIOBHAN   To put Mordaunt in the frame.

ANGELA stops dancing and looks directly at REBUS. Then she's gone.

REBUS   Right.

SIOBHAN   He'd just got away with rape and murder after all. A third woman dead. The same method as two other young women. You all *knew* Mordaunt did it. You just couldn't prove it. Must have been tempting to put him away for something?

REBUS   If we'd wanted to fix evidence to get Mordaunt we could have made a better job of it.

SIOBHAN   Maybe. Anyway, they do want to re-examine the forensic evidence from the attack on Cafferty.

REBUS   Has that been kept?

SIOBHAN   It has. Amazing I know, but it's still there
             and they know it.

REBUS   And what's that supposed to show?

SIOBHAN   DNA. Someone else's DNA. Not Mordaunt's.
             His defence team are going to claim that
             someone was so keen to get Mordaunt they
             framed him for the attack on Cafferty. Just
             so they could have the satisfaction of taking
             him off the streets. Putting him somewhere
             Cafferty might finish the job. But he didn't.
             And that's a puzzle isn't it?

REBUS   They're definitely re–examing the DNA
             evidence from the attack on Cafferty . . .?
             What would that even prove?

SIOBHAN   Oh like you can't see it! If the evidence
             shows Mordaunt didn't attack Cafferty it
             could suggest that the police might have
             been prepared to do anything to convict
             him. Then and now.

REBUS   Why would anyone even hold onto that
             evidence?! Case was solved. Cafferty
             deserved worse than a crack in his monster
             skull, and Mordaunt went down for it!

SIOBHAN   Maybe someone, somewhere in your team
             at the time, was uneasy with the quality of
             that conviction.

REBUS   Only thing that lot ever worried about was the quality of their porn mags and the size of their kick-backs.

SIOBHAN   John. Since we're here, since we're talking, I need to ask you . . .

REBUS   *(cuts her off)* No.

SIOBHAN   What?

REBUS   I never thought anyone on that squad tampered with evidence.

SIOBHAN   Seriously. Mordaunt is finally in our sights . . .

REBUS   Mordaunt is evil, rapist scum who preyed on girls who could barely walk out of school sandals.

SIOBHAN   But you never suspected anyone of framing him? Back then?

REBUS   No. Absolutely not.

SIOBHAN   And you'd tell me?

REBUS   Seriously. You need to ask me?

SIOBHAN   You know I do. I've put a lot into building the prosecution case here John, getting it in a proper state to match the modern forensic re-examination, making sure everything tallies . . .

REBUS   No-one I'd rather see picking up the baton
            than you.

SIOBHAN   And yes, it is this case. That's what's got me
            questioning everything. I'm at that point
            in my life John, the point where I'm asking
            what it's all worth. I've seen promotions fly
            past me before, I sometimes asked myself
            what I'm hanging in this job for . . .

REBUS   Because you're good at it.

SIOBHAN   Yes. It has to be because I'm good at it.
            Because I can get justice for a young girl,
            sixteen years old, twenty-five years dead,
            who just went out on a Friday night with
            her friends and died in pain and terror
            and shame before she ever really got to
            live. Now if I can't nail this bastard
            Mordaunt . . .

REBUS   You will.

SIOBHAN   If you know anything that might weaken
            our case against him . . .

REBUS   I'd never do that to you Shiv, never. I won't
            let that happen.

SIOBHAN slumps momentarily.

SIOBHAN   No. Course not. Alright. I need to get going.
            Are you really chasing up some bit of a
            murder case from 2001?

SIOBHAN is on the move.

REBUS   Fraser didn't re–interview a key witness,
            just filed the initial notes. I called him on it
            at the time.

SIOBHAN   I don't believe you really remembered that.

REBUS   *(showing her)* Here's the file, look.

SIOBHAN   John, I've got a live case, *now*. I can't
            even think about some cold case no-one
            remembers but you. *(checks herself)* Sorry,
            Sorry. I haven't slept. The case is water
            tight . . . but now the defence is saying they
            need more days on the trial schedule, more
            evidence to present. And I can only guess
            what it is . . .

REBUS   Well, you know how it works. You show
            yours but they never show theirs.

SIOBHAN   Even if they do want to drag in forensics
            from that assault case, it's convoluted, it's
            not enough to put up against what we've
            got. They must have something more. They
            must have a witness to that attack on
            Cafferty.

REBUS   Something like that, aye.

SIOBHAN catches his tone.

SIOBHAN   Which is my problem. *Not yours!* John?
               Promise me.

REBUS   Different world back then D.I. Clarke. You
               might not know the right stones to turn
               over.

SIOBHAN   You think I haven't been paying attention
               these last twenty-five years? Listen to me.
               Are you listening? Do not phone Cafferty.
               Promise me!

REBUS   Why would I talk to him?

SIOBHAN   Because you can't stand not knowing
               what's going on. Do not phone him. Do you
               hear me?

REBUS   I hear you.

SIOBHAN   Good.

She leaves. REBUS picks up his phone and dials. It connects.
Answer machine.

REBUS   Cafferty? It's me. Phone me.

He cuts the call. He looks at the file in his hand. MAGGIE
walks out of the shadows.

MAGGIE	Maggie Towler. Seventeen years old. Seventeen years dead. Are you going to do right by me now John? What's the hold up? I've been waiting since 2001.
REBUS	*(the file)* Aye . . . Aye, I need to chase this up . . .
MAGGIE	Oh don't make me laugh. You don't care. I'm just a distraction.
REBUS	I'm going to hunt this down. I don't forget. I never forget.

ANGELA is on, watching him.

ANGELA	Aren't you forgetting me?
REBUS	Siobhan's got you, Angela. She has. *(trying to convince himself)* Siobhan will get justice for you, Angela. So I need to . . . I need to . . .
MAGGIE	What?
REBUS	Keep moving. Sort this out. Come on Rebus. *(to MAGGIE)* I'll do better for you now Maggie. Promise.

The young women stand looking at him for another beat, then they're gone again. REBUS snatches up car keys and hurries out of the flat.

Stairwell Jackdaw pub

REBUS is climbing up as a BARMAN is carrying boxes of booze down the steps, struggling. REBUS is in his way.

BARMAN   Help you?

REBUS   You alright there?

BARMAN   Fuck no.

REBUS helps him, grabbing the top box as the barman nearly drops the lot, dumping them on the steps.

BARMAN   *(breathless)* Thanks.

REBUS   No bother.

BARMAN   See what it is, I always used to be able to carry three. So I just keep doing it. I'm no ready to say I'm not fit to carry three boxes. Do you think the booze is getting heavier? Is that it?

REBUS   Could be.

BARMAN   It might be. It's all the sugary shite they drink now. I'm sure it's got to weigh more. It's like treacle half of it.

REBUS   You've been here since it was a pub?

BARMAN Aye. Jackdaw pub. Still got the name. Still got me. Everything else has gone to shite. This used to be a real dockers' pub.

REBUS No more dockers.

BARMAN Extinct. Nothing but bankers, wankers and dockside redevelopment.

REBUS That didny really take did it?

BARMAN No round here. This place is still a dive, just got less smoke in it and louder music. I should sue the fuckers for industrial injury. See the way my heid pounds at the end of a Saturday night?

REBUS You still work behind the bar?

BARMAN Still do everything.

REBUS Still got regulars?

BARMAN Oh you see the same scabby wee faces . . .

REBUS Don't remember me though eh?

BARMAN You used to come in here?

REBUS Aye, a fair bit.

BARMAN If you say so.

REBUS *(the box)* Help you down with this?

BARMAN After you.

They move down with the boxes. REBUS still talking.

REBUS   Don't know that I've been in here this
         century mind you. Aye I have. You used to
         have a big screen tv in the bar there eh?

BARMAN   Aye.

REBUS   Aye that was it, January 2001. Raith
         Rovers got unlucky against Stirling Albion,
         terrible match . . .

BARMAN   That was on the big screen?

REBUS   *(ignoring that)* . . . That was no long before
         that poor lassie was killed here eh? Maggie
         Towler.

BARMAN   She wasny killed here.

REBUS   But she was drinking here that night eh?
         Only seventeen. Makes you think.

BARMAN   And she wouldny get in now. Is that what
         you're getting at? You police eh? We check
         ID. On the door. So if you're wanting to
         make issues about our license . . .

REBUS   Nothing like that. I'm no police.

BARMAN   Aye you are.

REBUS   Retired.

BARMAN   Aye. Right.

REBUS   So you remember her? Maggie Towler?

The BARMAN *is on the move again, laboriously hefting up his boxes.*

REBUS   And you saw her in here that night? You were working?

BARMAN   The fuck you're not polis. You want to know the answers you should have tried harder at the time.

REBUS   We should. You're not wrong.

BARMAN   No wonder you never caught the bastard.

REBUS   Which bastard.

BARMAN   The one that killed her.

REBUS   So who's that then?

A beat.

BARMAN   I don't need this kind of trouble any more.

REBUS   What kind of trouble?

BARMAN   We're closed and I'm busy.

The BARMAN *is nearly away.*

REBUS   You think you know who did it.

BARMAN   No. I don't. But I know she was scared of him. And I know you bastards didny even ask the right questions.

REBUS   So what would be the right question?

BARMAN   Maggie didny scare easy.

REBUS   So who scared her?

BARMAN   Wasny just a random guy leaping on her in the dark. It was someone she knew. She ran out of here because she saw someone who'd already scared her. Seventeen years and you still don't know why? Guy like you wrote it all down. Go and ask him.

REBUS   Where did she die?

BARMAN   Building site just across the street there. It's a high rise now, dockside redevelopment. You can't even see the ground where they found her.

BARMAN leaves.

Granton high rise

REBUS is looking up. MAGGIE joins him. As always she's only in his mind's eye.

MAGGIE   So you do care. I'm touched. You think you know the stones to turn over, John?

REBUS starts to climb.

MAGGIE   In seventeen years most of the stones have been dug up. They've had concrete poured over them, car parks built on them, glass towers and gentrified tenements squeezing out the dark underworld that scuttled under the surface of the douce capital's streets . . . Oh but the dark's still there, isn't it John?

REBUS is climbing up.

MAGGIE   They marked my grave with great towers. High rises with balconies in the clouds, sold to dreamers that believed they'd sit in the sky watching the sparkling silver sea laid out below . . . And the sharp east wind drives the grey Forth onto the glass.

REBUS is looking out over the view.

REBUS   What scared you Maggie? Someone you
         knew you couldny handle.

MAGGIE   I'm seventeen John, I think I can take on
         the world.

REBUS   Someone we never even questioned,
         because we didny do our job. We didny
         know he was there. Why was he there? And
         why did no-one see him?

*REBUS is going quickly downstairs again. MAGGIE follows
him.*

MAGGIE   What makes you think you'll see it now?

REBUS   Because it's in here. All in my head. I don't
         forget.

ANGELA is suddenly there too, talking to MAGGIE.

ANGELA   He does forget. He's forgetting me.

MAGGIE   He's only doing this to forget you.

ANGELA   I know.

REBUS is trying to think, stopped at the foot of the stairs.

ANGELA   Siobhan will nail my killer and you'll find
         Maggie's. That'd be nice.

MAGGIE   That'd be very nice.

ANGELA   Except he hasn't told Siobhan everything.

MAGGIE   And no-one saw me fall John . . . Except the
          man that pushed me down. What are you
          trying to remember?

REBUS   A name . . .

MAGGIE   You better hope it's the name of a man
          that's still alive. You spend too much time
          talking to the dead these days, eh John?

REBUS   Got it!

        Quick transition into—

A pub

Scuzzy, old–school drinking dive. A small man in a bunnet is nursing a pint and chaser. He startles as he sees REBUS *moving towards him but* REBUS *blocks him before he can leave.* REBUS *is already carrying drinks.*

REBUS   You running off with half your drink still on the bar Charlie? That's no like you.

CHARLIE   What do you want Rebus?

REBUS   *(offering glass)* To buy you the other half of that.

CHARLIE   I'm no talking to you. You're no even a policeman anymore. I don't have to tell you anything.

REBUS   *(the drink)* So you don't want this?

CHARLIE   What are you doing in here?

REBUS   Just looking for a bar that's no been turned into a bistro. You canny get a drink in this town any more without some floppy haired article offering you a tapas menu.

CHARLIE   Aye you're no wrong there.

CHARLIE accepts the drink.

REBUS   This place is holding out though.

CHARLIE   Just about.

REBUS   The Hebrides isny too bad.

CHARLIE   *(snorts)* You're joking eh? Full of foreigners
            and fucking backpackers.

REBUS   Oh I'll tell you where's ruined. The
            Jackdaw, down in Newhaven.

CHARLIE   *(not really interested)* That right? No been
            down there in years.

REBUS   Did you no used to drink down there?

CHARLIE   Mebbe when I was working down there
            but . . .

REBUS   *(cutting in)* Working down there? Doing
            what?

CHARLIE   Rebus, what do you think I do?

REBUS   Five to ten for aggravated burglary usually.

CHARLIE   *(dignity)* I have a trade. I am a craftsman.

REBUS   Is that right?

CHARLIE   *(handing him a card)* I am a signed–up member
            of the Federation of Master Builders. Any
            home improvement, I'm your man.

REBUS   You do extensions and loft conversions and
            all that?

CHARLIE   My speciality.

REBUS   Right enough, great way to case the better
              quality home.

CHARLIE   Fuck yo, Rebus.

REBUS   That what you were doing in Newhaven?

CHARLIE   I don't need to talk to you.

REBUS   So you keep saying.

CHARLIE   I was nothing but legit then. Didny need to
              worry about money, building never stopped
              then.

REBUS   You worked on the flats down there?

CHARLIE   You could name your price. They were
              throwing those flats up so fast . . .

REBUS   Happy days eh?

CHARLIE   They didn't use marine grade on one single
              fixture or fitting. Not one. That sea wind
              has turned every block into a subsiding
              monster leaking rust from every hole.

REBUS   So you were working there when that lassie
              got strangled.

CHARLIE   Maggie Towler. Aye. I knew her.

REBUS   You knew her?

CHARLIE   Just to look at. She was a looker, wee
              Maggie. Know what got her killed?

REBUS   Tell me.

CHARLIE   Shagging above her pay grade.

REBUS   Go on.

CHARLIE   That's it. Word was she was having a
           flingette with one of the developers.

REBUS   The property developers?

CHARLIE   That's right.

REBUS   Name?

CHARLIE   I don't know that! If I'd known that I'd've
           told you lot at the time. That was horrible
           what that monster did to wee Maggie.

REBUS   So how did you know about it?

CHARLIE   Must have heard someone talking about it
           on the site.

REBUS   Who?

CHARLIE   I don't know! Half of them were Polish
           anyway.

REBUS   What was the name of the property
           company?

CHARLIE thinks for a moment.

CHARLIE   Weston? No, that's no right. It began with
           an E . . .

REBUS takes out a note and hands it to him.

REBUS   When it comes to you, phone me.

CHARLIE   Why would I do that?

REBUS   There's another of those coming to you if
             you give me the name.

CHARLIE   Google it.

REBUS snatches the note back.

REBUS   Fuck, you're right. Thanks Charlie.

REBUS is on the move. CHARLIE shouts after him.

CHARLIE   You tight bastard! I'm glad Ger Cafferty's
             going to fuck you over!

REBUS is right back on him. He grabs his hand, hard.

REBUS   What's that?

CHARLIE   Nothing.

REBUS   Charlie, don't make me hurt these skilled
             craftsman's fingers.

CHARLIE   *(agony)* Fuck off you bastard! You'll get us
             both barred!

REBUS   Then stop screaming. What was that about
             Big Ger?

CHARLIE   He said he was going to fuck you over.

REBUS   He's been saying that for thirty years. Said
          it to who?

CHARLIE   I might have heard him.

REBUS   Where was this?

CHARLIE   I was just lifting a motor he wanted
          shifted . . .

REBUS   When?

CHARLIE   Couple of months back mebbe . . . end of
          last year? I don't fucking know, you bastard!
          Let go!

REBUS   Know what you are? A wee dug trying to
          borrow a big dog's bark. Cafferty wouldn't
          lift his leg to piss on you.

REBUS lets CHARLIE go and walks out onto—

Stairwell, Arden Street

At the foot of the stairs REBUS *takes out his phone and punches the number. It's answered almost at once.*

REBUS   Cafferty, need to have a word . . .

He stops abruptly as, voiced by MAGGIE, *we hear what he hears.*

PHONE   The number you've dialled has not been recognised. The number you've dialled has not been recognised.

REBUS *stares at it, checking the number. Then he cuts the call and slowly climbs the stairs.* ANDY *is coming down. He checks when he sees* REBUS.

REBUS   Where's your friend?

ANDY   What do you want?

REBUS   I need to talk to her, it's about her mother. I need her number. Come on. Your pal, Heather Ross.

ANDY   Who?

REBUS   Oh don't play games with me son.

ANDY *tries to pass him.* REBUS *blocks him.*

ANDY   Fuck off! I'm warning you . . .

REBUS   What you going to do? Call the police?
              You'll no do that will you Andy?

ANDY   I said fuck off!

*ANDY shoves REBUS and REBUS suddenly has him pinned
against the wall.*

REBUS   You think I couldn't push you through this
              wall, Andy? Now you listen. First thing,
              you're moving out. Give notice, get going, I
              don't care where you go to peddle your sad
              wee packets of skunk but you'll take it off
              my stair and if I see you even put your nose
              round the door I'll have you in a cell before
              you've a chance to sniff.

ANDY   I'm not dealing . . .

REBUS   *(shaking him)* Are you packing your bags?

ANDY   Yes.

REBUS   Good. And I'll let you. Once you give me
              Heather's number.

ANDY   I don't . . .

His tone is suddenly more subdued.

ANDY   I don't phone her. She phones me. Number
              withheld.

REBUS   Smart girl.

He's on the move.

REBUS   Start packing.

ANDY goes back into his flat, REBUS moves into—

Rebus's Arden Street flat

*CAFFERTY is sitting in his chair, watching the door. A
moment as REBUS takes this in.*

REBUS   Ghosts.

CAFFERTY   Don't believe in them.

REBUS   I've spent half the day chasing them.

CAFFERTY   So I heard.

REBUS   You've changed your number.

CAFFERTY   I have. Don't you want to know how I got
               in?

REBUS   Doesny take a master criminal. And I've
               nothing to steal.

CAFFERTY holds up keys.

CAFFERTY   You'll be needing these back.

REBUS   No. I'm thinking of changing the locks.

CAFFERTY   Reckon that'll stop me?

REBUS   Just ring the bell Big Ger. Mi casa, su casa,
               all that.

CAFFERTY   I've no even had the offer of a cup of tea yet.
               What kind of a welcome is that?

REBUS   There's no milk.

CAFFERTY holds up a half pint.

CAFFERTY   Looks like I'm a better detective than you
             Strawman.

REBUS   I'll put the kettle on.

REBUS leaves the room. CAFFERTY is prowling, inspecting it.

CAFFERTY   No been here for a while. Nothing's changed
             though eh? No even the dust.

REBUS   *(off)* Canny get the staff.

CAFFERTY   I could recommend a couple of great
             women. Nae stour too hard to lift.

REBUS   Scrubbing bloodstains out of Persian rugs?

CAFFERTY   Nothing like that. Everything clean and
             sparkling in my world John, that's the way
             I like it.

REBUS is back on.

REBUS   So I'm off your Christmas card list am I?
             What did I do? Something really annoying I
             hope . . .

CAFFERTY   It was time.

REBUS   Time for what?

CAFFERTY   We'll get to that. Why did you want to get hold of me?

REBUS   Wanted to ask you something.

CAFFERTY   About the Mordaunt trial?

REBUS   Among other things.

CAFFERTY   You lot have taken your time eh? Twenty-five years to finally get that poisonous arse wipe in the dock again.

REBUS   You're looking forward to a result then?

CAFFERTY   *(ignoring the question)* Twenty-five years. 1992 eh? John Major, royal divorces, Ravenscraig closes for good, IRA bombs . . . You could still see over your own belly. You could probably still run upstairs back then, eh John? Let's get in the mood. You got any music from 1992?

REBUS   Nothing to your taste.

CAFFERTY   I'm going to tell you something now that'll surprise you.

REBUS   Should I record it?

CAFFERTY   I've always been a bit of a Sheena Easton fan. You got any Sheena Easton?

REBUS   Strangely enough I haven't.

CAFFERTY   Now there's a woman with the X Factor. I
           met her once. On a chat show.

REBUS   She was promoting her new album. You
           were promoting your memoir of murder
           and mayhem . . .

CAFFERTY   You read it yet?

REBUS   Do you need to ask?

CAFFERTY   Keeps me in fine wine and classy company
           John. Did I tell you I've got a wine
           cellar now? A wine room to be accurate.
           Temperature controlled environment.

REBUS   Stops the bodies decomposing does it?

CAFFERTY   Wine is an investment, John. Something
           you should have considered before they
           kicked you into touch. Still, some of this old
           vinyl's worth a bit these days they tell me.

REBUS   You canny put a price on memories.

CAFFERTY   True. And we've got our share eh John?
           1992. Not a year I remember so well as it
           turned out. I was in intensive care for a bit
           of it.

REBUS   But Mordaunt paid for that.

CAFFERTY   And now it's time for him to pay for the rest
           of it. We should have a proper drink to that
           eh?

REBUS   I'm pacing myself these days.

CAFFERTY   You're no fun these days John, that's the
                 truth. Will you go to the trial?

REBUS   I don't know.

CAFFERTY   I'll be there. There's a fascination eh?
                 Staring at a man you know is a piece of
                 pure evil. Don't look at me like that, I never
                 killed any civilians. And I wouldn't even
                 breathe the same air as a sick wee bastard
                 like Mordaunt. Useless plumber as well. I
                 ended up with raw sewage leaking into the
                 jacuzzi. Subsidence my arse. Wee scumbag
                 barely knew how to lag a pipe.

REBUS   You're going to the trial?

CAFFERTY   Beats daytime television. Have you seen
                 'Homes under the Hammer'?

REBUS   I know where I'd like to put the hammer.

CAFFERTY   What are you doing with yourself all day,
                 when you're not looking for me?

REBUS   I keep busy.

CAFFERTY   Talking to ghosts. So what did you want to
                 ask me?

REBUS   Have Mordaunt's defence team contacted
                 you?

CAFFERTY   Now. Why would you be asking that?
              Mordaunt dunts me on the heid in 1992
              and you think his defence might want to
              talk to me? Prosecution maybe . . . but the
              defence? What would put an idea like that
              in your head?

REBUS   Have they?

CAFFERTY   Maybe they have. How did you guess that?

REBUS   Maybe I'm still a detective after all.

CAFFERTY   In which case you shouldn't be talking to
              me, should you?

REBUS   What are you playing at Cafferty? Why
              would you help Mordaunt? What's in it for
              you?

CAFFERTY   I can think of almost nothing on this earth
              I'd enjoy more than seeing that piece of filth
              nailed down so he canny get up for the rest
              of his shrivelled wee life.

REBUS   So what are you doing?

CAFFERTY   Almost nothing I'd enjoy more.

   REBUS realises.

REBUS   It's you isn't it? Shit it's you. You're the
              mystery witness for the defence!

CAFFERTY   How could I help Mordaunt, the man who attacked me?

REBUS   By saying it wasny him that attacked you at all! This is your idea of a game is it? You know this is the conviction half of Police Scotland have wanted for twenty-five years and you're going to piss on our bonfire, just for the hell of it?

CAFFERTY   I never saw who attacked me. Did I? He was a cowardly piece of shite that whacked me when my back was turned. But I don't like the idea the wrong cowardly shite took the rap for that John. That offends my sense of justice.

REBUS   Your sense of what?

CAFFERTY *is on the move.*

CAFFERTY   Listen. This is a bigger conversation. I'm running late. Places to go, people to see, you know how it is. Keeping busy. Why don't you come over to my place tonight? Come and see the view. Let me repay your extravagant hospitality. Spot of dinner at mine.

REBUS   Dinner parties? What's next? Saga cruises and National Trust membership?

CAFFERTY   There's a working lift, no worries about
            getting your old legs up to the seventh floor.
            Home delivery from a Michelin starred
            chef . . .

REBUS   Stop fucking playing with me and tell me
            what's going on!

CAFFERTY   I hope you've got someone keeping an eye
            on your blood pressure John, you've gone a
            terrible colour there. Come round tonight.
            I'll explain the deal then.

REBUS   What deal? I'm not making deals with you.

CAFFERTY   You don't have to. Seven for seven thirty.
            Alright? You know where I am, no need to
            bring a bottle. I'm well sorted.

REBUS   Aye and you'll be well sorted out when I
            fill the defence team in on the quality of
            their witness. I don't think a man who's
            never knowingly embraced the truth in any
            court of law is going to make much of a star
            witness. Do you?

CAFFERTY   See, the way I heard it . . . there's some
            suspicion the police have a habit of getting
            a bit creative with evidence, in their
            natural eagerness to see Mordaunt go
            down. The defence is going to ask for a re-
            examination of the DNA evidence from the
            attack on me. But you knew that, didn't

you? It's an amazing thing, isn't it an amazing thing? They've still got the stick of wood the guy whacked me with. Stupid bastard kicked it under a car two streets away. Careless, might have been pissed. Do you think he was maybe pissed John? They've got tiny tiny traces from that stick, wee scales of skin, that's all they need now – wee scales of skin from whoever held that bit of wood twenty-five years ago, and then they'll know who he is. And if it wasn't Mordaunt that'll raise a few questions about the quality of *all* the forensic evidence eh? Most dust is actually human skin scales. Did you know that? You should buy a hoover John, you're choking on DNA in here.

CAFFERTY is almost gone.

REBUS   A court's already decided who hit you Ger, it was Mordaunt.

CAFFERTY   That's no who I saw.

REBUS   You didny see anyone.

CAFFERTY   How do you know?

REBUS   You said you couldn't see your attacker.

CAFFERTY   I couldny remember at first. I was laid up
            in the Royal Infirmary with a crack in my
            heid.

REBUS   But now it's all coming back to you. It's a
            miracle.

CAFFERTY   Think what you like but basically I'm an
            honest man John. I don't have to lie my way
            out of trouble. Always thought that was a
            sign of weakness.

REBUS   So be honest. You never saw his face. Did
            you?

CAFFERTY   No.

REBUS   Then stop playing your games and let us
            get a clear shot at Mordaunt . . .

CAFFERTY   I didny need to see his face. I saw his shoes.
            Last thing I saw before it all went dark.
            Beautiful polished shoes. Shoes buffed to a
            shine only a man with the army in his DNA
            could ever bring off. I saw my dying face in
            those shoes John. Or I thought I did. I'm
            prepared to swear I would have recognised
            them anywhere.

He's looking at REBUS*'S shoes.*

CAFFERTY   Let's have a look at your shoes John?
            No *quite* as shiny these days. Ah well.

Standards are slipping. Nothing's quite what it was in 1992 but the memories live on. As we started so we'll finish. But I think it's my turn to give the killer blow. Eh John? I'll see you tonight and I'll tell you the deal. Smart casual, what you're wearing's fine. Don't even need to buff up your shoes.

CAFFERTY leaves. REBUS is frozen. ANGELA walks out of the dark and looks at him, reproachful.

ANGELA   You weren't paying attention John, were you? You'll have no time for me and Maggie now, will you? It's all about your secrets now eh? Poor wee dead Maggie. No justice for her today. No justice for her or me any day.

There's a scream off.

HEATHER   *(off stage)* Shit! No! Nooooo!

REBUS moves quickly into—

Stairwell, Arden Street

ANDY is crawling down the stairs, bleeding. He collapses.
REBUS hurries to him. Checking him. He's phoning. HEATHER
appears further up the stairs, she's in bits.

HEATHER   Look at him! Look!

REBUS   *(on phone)* Police and ambulance . . . possible
               assault . . . 17 Arden Street . . .

HEATHER comes slowly down the stairs, staring at ANDY in
horror.

REBUS   *(on phone)* I don't know. He's bleeding out,
               multiple stab wounds . . . Just get here!

REBUS is trying to stop the bleeding. It's too late. HEATHER
is backing off down the stairs, horrified.

HEATHER   He's dead isn't he? He's dead . . .

HEATHER is running.

REBUS   Heather wait . . . Heather . . . *Heather*!

She's gone. REBUS crouches over ANDY'S body.

Act Two

Rebus's Arden Street flat/dream

REBUS puts a record on, 'Take the Weather' by Crowded House. He stands looking out the window, listening to it. ANGELA steps out of the shadows, dancing, laughing.

ANGELA   You can't dance to this!

She's not talking to REBUS but he answers her.

REBUS   No.

ANGELA is looking at someone else. MORDAUNT steps out of the dark, smiling at ANGELA. Like the young woman he's not really there.

MORDAUNT   You can. Not many girls with the confidence to dance on their own like that. You know you look good eh?

ANGELA stops dancing.

MORDAUNT   Don't stop. Aw I've put you off. Sorry. Didny mean to stare. It's just you're a really good dancer. Are you a professional?

ANGELA   *(laughing)* What? No!

MORDAUNT   Not many girls with the confidence to dance
            on their own like that. You know you look
            good eh?

ANGELA   It's just boring sitting drinking. I'd rather
            dance.

MORDAUNT   I can't. Bad leg. My sister does though.
            She's training to be a dancer. You could get
            on a course like hers. She started out here
            and now she's dancing in London.

ANGELA   For real?

MORDAUNT   Aye, come and meet her, she's just outside
            having a fag.

ANGELA hesitates.

ANGELA   I can't leave my friends . . .

MORDAUNT   Aye come on. She clocked you earlier. She
            thinks you're a great dancer too. Just come
            outside for a quick word.

*MORDAUNT is leading ANGELA into the shadows. REBUS
moves to stop them. But MORDAUNT is suddenly gone and
ANGELA turns on him, attacking.*

ANGELA   What are you going to do John? Stop him?
            Save me?

REBUS   I can't.

ANGELA   No. You can't. He already did his worst. It was horrible John. So horrible. I was so frightened, he hurt me so much, and I just prayed and prayed and begged to live . . . But I didn't. He killed me. It wasn't quick and I knew I was dying.

REBUS   He won't get away with it. I won't let it happen.

ANGELA   If he does, it's on you John. Your fault!

Rebus's Arden Street flat/dawn

REBUS wakes abruptly in an armchair. ANGELA is gone. A young woman DETECTIVE is sitting opposite him, taking his statement.

DETECTIVE   Are we keeping you up, Mr Rebus?

REBUS   Sorry, just . . . long night.

DETECTIVE   Sun's coming up now.

REBUS   *(looking)* So it is.

DETECTIVE   So . . . you believe the deceased, Andrew Lamont to have been dealing drugs . . .

REBUS   Just low key I think, wee packets of skunk to get him better drinking money, maybe pills for the weekend ravers but . . .

DETECTIVE   *(cutting in)* And you didn't report this?

REBUS   No. I dealt with it.

DETECTIVE   Dealt with it?

REBUS   I'd moved him on. *(as she stares at him accusingly)* Look, I don't know what success rate the drugs squad are getting from busting wee dope heids these days, but when you want to catch the big fish, in my day, you . . .

DETECTIVE   *(cutting him off)* Aye I'm guessing there's a lot
             different from your day.

REBUS   Look, you don't want to believe all the
             stories you hear about me, I . . .

DETECTIVE   *(cutting him off again)* What stories? I've not
             heard any stories. I didn't know you'd ever
             been a policeman till you told me Mr Rebus.

REBUS   When did you join the force?

DETECTIVE   Five years ago.

REBUS   You don't look old enough.

DETECTIVE   And you don't know anything else about
             the other witness, Heather Ross?

REBUS   She's Maggie Towler's daughter.

DETECTIVE   Who?

REBUS   A murder. Before your time. Everyone's
             forgotten except me. And wee Heather.

The DETECTIVE *is on the move.*

DETECTIVE   Well if you see 'wee Heather' again, tell her
             we're needing a word. Were you planning
             on going anywhere this morning sir?

REBUS   Don't know yet.

DETECTIVE   Well can I ask you to wait in for a few
             hours. My boss might want another word.

REBUS   Who's your boss?

DETECTIVE   D.I. Mackie.

REBUS   Don't know him.

DETECTIVE   Her. No she didn't know you either.

*The DETECTIVE leaves. ANGELA is back in the room
watching REBUS.*

ANGELA   You think Cafferty had that boy gutted
             on your doorstep. A calling card. A wee
             reminder of all he is. Why didn't you tell
             the nice police lady that John?

She follows REBUS as he moves restlessly.

ANGELA   I know why. You're a man with dangerous
             secrets. Have to save yourself eh John? But
             what about me? And Maggie? And Heather?
             Canny save all of us, Rebus.

REBUS   The fuck I can't.

He snatches up car keys, quick transition into—

Forensic lab, Fettes Police H.Q.

REBUS is facing a wall of bagged evidence. A lab
TECHNICIAN is bustling past, busy with his work.

TECHNICIAN   You can't be in here.

REBUS   I get that a lot.

The TECHNICIAN moves off as MAGGIE and ANGELA are on.
They are reciting the contents of the evidence bags.

MAGGIE   Bloostained shirt. 1978.

ANGELA   Gerald Moore. Stabbed. Unsolved murder.

MAGGIE   2009. An adjustable spanner, brain matter
             and partial finger prints.

ANGELA   Susan Hickman. Coshed and left for dead.
             Assailant unknown.

MAGGIE   A pair of tights . . .

ANGELA   My tights . . .

MAGGIE   Trace DNA inside the knots, a tiny record
             of the fingers that pulled the knots tight . . .
             tight . . .

ANGELA   A indian silk scarf . . .

MAGGIE   My scarf . . .

ANGELA   Trace DNA on the folds, a tiny record of the
               fingers that pulled it tight . . . tight . . .

MAGGIE   A piece of building timber . . .

ANGELA   Morris Gerald Cafferty's blood . . .

MAGGIE   And a tiny record of the hands that lifted
               that cosh and swung it . . . *hard* . . .

ANGELA   What would you do, even if they let you see
               it John?

MAGGIE   Steal it?

ANGELA   If he can just break the seal on the bag it'll
               be useless in court.

MAGGIE   Is that the plan?

ANGELA   Christ that's a useless plan. He'll get
               caught.

REBUS moves restlessly.

REBUS   *(to himself)* Fuck's sake hold it together.

MAGGIE and ANGELA are gone. The TECHNICIAN is back.

TECHNICIAN I said you can't be in here.

REBUS   Is Josie about?

TECHNICIAN Who?

REBUS   Josie Cassidy? Technician here?

TECHNICIAN	Took maternity leave two years ago and never came back.
REBUS	How could she give all this up?
TECHNICIAN	Like I said, you need a visitor's pass to be in here.
REBUS	Sorry son, we've not met before have we? D.I. Rebus.
TECHNICIAN	I'd need to see some ID.
REBUS	Retired.
TECHNICIAN	Then you have to leave.
REBUS	Aye, course, just one quick question . . .
TECHNICIAN	No, you really have to leave . . .
REBUS	How is Josie?
TECHNICIAN	*(thrown)* Eh . . .
REBUS	What did she have? Boy, girl?
TECHNICIAN	I think it was twins actually.
REBUS	Jeezo . . . she couldny have been more than four foot high.
TECHNICIAN	I know . . .
REBUS	God, must have been like a weeble wobble woman the last month. Did she work to the end? 'Cause she never liked the busy days anyway did she?

TECHNICIAN No . . .

REBUS   Days like today with half the town's
           lawyers and polis in keeping an eye on
           where the evidence is going. Have they
           been in to pick up the Mordaunt evidence
           yet?

TECHNICIAN Eh . . . *(he's flustered checking paperwork)* That
           went down last week I think . . .

REBUS   No. Different case. Not the rape/murder.
           The defence wants to look at the evidence
           from the assault Mordaunt was convicted of
           in 1992. Has that gone down yet?

           SIOBHAN *enters. Not pleased to see* REBUS.

SIOBHAN   What're you doing here? You can't be in
           here.

TECHNICIAN I told him.

REBUS   Just catching up on news of Josie and the
           kids.

SIOBHAN   Who?

REBUS   *(to* TECHNICIAN*)* See? No-one has time for the
           personal stuff any more.

SIOBHAN   What are you doing here John?

REBUS   What're you doing here?

SIOBHAN   I work here.

REBUS   In forensic storage?

A beat.

SIOBHAN   Tom, can you tell me if anyone's picked up the evidence to be tested for court 9? An assault on Morris Gerald Cafferty in 1992.

TECHNICIAN   That's just what he was asking.

SIOBHAN   Is that so? Well, has it been picked up?

TECHNICIAN   *(checking)* Yup. That went on its way this morning.

SIOBHAN   Good. Glad to hear it. No-one else had a look at it before it went did they?

TECHNICIAN   No.

SIOBHAN   Just checking. Sorry to bother you. Got time for a word John?

REBUS   I'm glad you're here D.I. Clarke. Tell him.

SIOBHAN   Tell him what?

REBUS   We need to check the evidence for Maggie Towler's murder.

SIOBHAN is just staring at him.

REBUS   March, 2001. Building site between Granton and Newhaven. Lead detective D.I. Morris. *(as no-one moves)* Case number 4568/NM/ Morris.

SIOBHAN   *(to TECHNICIAN)* Can you look please?

TECHNICIAN   What am I checking?

REBUS   That it's still there, safe, sealed and fit for court.

The TECHNICIAN moves off.

REBUS   And once we've done that we need to get the name of the property company that developed those flats . . .

SIOBHAN   We're not doing anything John. I've been over this.

REBUS   Right. Fine. I'll get it all together myself. Hand it over to you with a big bow tied round the case . . .

SIOBHAN   What case!?

REBUS   Maggie Towler. I told you. She's the unsolved from seventeen years ago? I met her daughter, Heather, night before last. She was on my stair.

SIOBHAN   What was she doing there?

REBUS   Don't know. She vanished on me.

SIOBHAN   You can have that effect on people.

REBUS   But I remembered we let mother her down.

SIOBHAN   And that's why you're here?

REBUS   Of course that's why I'm here. Why else would I be here?

SIOBHAN   So why were you asking about the Mordaunt evidence?

REBUS   Just making conversation. It's on my mind Siobhan. What can I tell you? Why were you here? Just checking no-one had tried tampering with the Mordaunt evidence?

SIOBHAN   Yes.

REBUS   Well there you go. Nothing to worry about.

SIOBHAN   You have to stop John . . .

REBUS   Stop what?

SIOBHAN   Poking into cold cases.

REBUS   Oh so Maggie Towler doesny deserve justice?

SIOBHAN   Will she get it if you steam in trampling all over the evidence . . .?

She's cut off as the TECHNICIAN is back.

TECHNICIAN   Still there. Sealed, safe and ready for court.

SIOBHAN   Thank you.

TECHNICIAN No problem. *(indicating REBUS)* But he
           shouldn't be in here.

SIOBHAN   I'll walk him out.

The TECHNICIAN leaves as SIOBHAN walks REBUS into—

Stairwell Police H.Q.

SIOBHAN   Have you slept?

REBUS   Have you?

He puts something in his mouth.

SIOBHAN   What's that? You trying the nicotine
               lozenges?

REBUS   Had to try something.

SIOBHAN   What do they taste like?

REBUS   Well I've never actually licked an ashtray
               full of cat's piss but . . .

SIOBHAN   We've got a family liason officer visiting
               Angela's father. But I promised him I'd
               keep him informed personally. I took
               his hand and looked him in the eye and
               promised him I'd convict the man that
               destroyed his daughter twenty five years
               ago . . . Destroyed him too. He's just a husk
               of a man, a living container of unbearable
               grief.

REBUS   No mother?

SIOBHAN   Cancer. Five years ago. They'd split up by
               then.

REBUS	Sorrow too heavy for two to carry. See it all the time.
SIOBHAN	We have to get Mordaunt convicted John. We have to.
REBUS	I know.
SIOBHAN	And there's something you're not telling me.
REBUS	Right.
SIOBHAN	Isn't there?
REBUS	Mebbe.
SIOBHAN	Something to do with the attack on Big Ger. Who are you protecting John?
REBUS	You.
SIOBHAN	From what?
REBUS	A mess. A mess that you don't need to worry about.
SIOBHAN	Oh dear god . . . *(she slumps)* You rang him didn't you?
REBUS	He came round the flat.
SIOBHAN	I know. We've got a tail on him.
REBUS	*(genuine)* Smart girl . . .
SIOBHAN	Oh don't even start with that! Don't you . . . !

REBUS	What? It was the right thing to do.
SIOBHAN	Yes John, I know, because I'm a *really good detective*.
REBUS	You want to know what we talked about.
SIOBHAN	Are you going to tell me?
REBUS	He's got nothing Shiv. It's all a bluff. He's just messing with your head. Last night? He just fancied tormenting me.
SIOBHAN	Is he going in the witness box?
REBUS	Not unless he wants to look like a clown. Big Ger will not mess up your case against Mordaunt. You can keep staring at me Siobhan but you're either going to trust me on this or you're not.
SIOBHAN	If I couldn't trust you on something like this I wouldn't trust this job, I wouldn't trust myself, I wouldn't trust any seeming solid thing in the whole world.

A beat.

REBUS	No pressure then.
SIOBHAN	Something I've always wanted to ask you: why does Cafferty call you 'Strawman'?
REBUS	I was giving evidence against him in a case in Glasgow, the lawyer got me mixed

up with another witness called 'Stroman'. Cafferty loves that.

SIOBHAN   He thinks you're a man of straw.

REBUS   He wishes I was.

SIOBHAN   And you think you're a lone wolf. The last gunslinger in High Noon, taking down the bad guys as he goes.

REBUS   What do you think I am?

SIOBHAN   Retired. And good police work is team work John.

REBUS   You think? I think a result's a result.

SIOBHAN   John . . .

REBUS   *(cutting in)* I hear you Siobhan. I do.

SIOBHAN   I see her you know. In my head.

REBUS   Who?

SIOBHAN   Angela. Just watching me. Never had that before on a murder, not even my first. I see her. Staring at me. Asking if I'm going to get her the only thing worth anything to her now. A bit of justice, for that little life snapped short . . .

MAGGIE and ANGELA are on.

REBUS   I know. I see her too. I remember watching Sam going out for a night with her pals at that age.

SIOBHAN   How is she?

REBUS   Good, pestering me to come and see the granddaughter before she's taller than Sam is.

SIOBHAN   Well you've the time now.

REBUS   That's what she says. In a few years that toddler will be a teenager. Then Sam will understand what it was like, looking at her, so fresh and full of life, beautiful . . . and fragile as a moth. She didn't understand why I shouted at her for pulling her top down and making up her face like she was something glossy and available. She didn't see what I saw . . . what the predatory monsters out there would see. Christ. The way young lassies dress themselves up Shiv . . .

SIOBHAN   A young woman's got every right . . .

REBUS   *(cutting her off)* Aye I know I know.

SIOBHAN   Attacks like the one on Angela, on Maggie Towler are rare. Still. Women risk more in their own homes. Young women can't be prisoners of their father's fears . . .

REBUS	It is just a fact that a strong man can grab a woman and do whatever he likes. It's just a fact that young women will always need protection, as long as that's true. And we're the protection, or we should be. We need to get them locked up.
SIOBHAN	Maybe the answer is to keep trying to make a world where no man ever would hurt a young woman.

REBUS is surrendering something, realising he can't fix this, struggling with that.

REBUS	Aye. Alright. Alright.
SIOBHAN	What?
REBUS	I can't see a way through . . .
SIOBHAN	What is it?
REBUS	Shiv . . . There's maybe is something I do need to talk to you about . . .

She waits. He can't find a way to go on.

SIOBHAN	Well what is it?
REBUS	Nothing. No it's nothing. I'll fix it myself. Just . . . Look . . . I might need your help, tonight . . .
SIOBHAN	*(cutting him off)* Oh I can't tonight.

REBUS	*(thrown)* Oh. Right. Sorry.
SIOBHAN	No I'm going out. I have to . . . I mean I want to eh . . . *(she's floundering)* It's just this thing . . .
REBUS	*(cutting in)* Hot date?
SIOBHAN	Hardly. Important. Important date.
REBUS	Anyone I know?
SIOBHAN	It's work. I can't shift it so . . .
REBUS	No, no, fine. Work on the Mordaunt trial?

She says nothing.

REBUS	'Course it is. And nothing you can tell me . . .
SIOBHAN	Sorry, it's just . . .
REBUS	I'm no even asking. It's fine. Really.
SIOBHAN	I could come and see you after? How late will you be up? Stupid question . . .
REBUS	*(cutting her off)* No, I'll be out. I thought maybe you could come with but . . .
SIOBHAN	How about I buy you breakfast?
REBUS	Aye . . . aye that might work.
SIOBHAN	You can tell me all about it then.
REBUS	Yeah. Alright. I'll tell you all about it then.

SIOBHAN   It's a date.

She's on the move, going back upstairs.

REBUS   So you know about the murder on my stair
            then?

She pauses.

REBUS   If you had eyes on me and Cafferty then
            you'll have heard about the murder on my
            stair? *(as she doesn't reply)* Why didn't you
            say?

SIOBHAN   I was waiting to see when you'd tell me. You
            fancy Cafferty for that?

REBUS   Don't you?

SIOBHAN   So why didn't you tell that very competent
            police officer who interviewed you?

REBUS   I'll tell you at breakfast.

SIOBHAN   You better.

*SIOBHAN goes back upstairs. REBUS walks slowly down the
stairs. ANGELA and MAGGIE are with him.*

MAGGIE   You couldn't tell her.

ANGELA   Couldn't face it.

MAGGIE   Well that's just weak!

REBUS   Fucking shut it!

Transition into—

Rebus's Arden Street flat

REBUS is searching through paperwork, not even sure what he's looking for. MAGGIE and ANGELA are still with him, still talking. REBUS has put music on, we barely hear it, it's HEATHER and MAGGIE's song 'Show Me the Way'.

ANGELA   Look at him, did you really think he cared about us? It's all about her.

MAGGIE   Siobhan . . . We're dead.

ANGELA   No sense worrying about the dead.

MAGGIE   But if Siobhan Clarke finds out you lied to her . . .

ANGELA   Messed with her . . .

MAGGIE   Let her down . . .

REBUS shouts at them, at the world.

REBUS   Cafferty's got nothing!

MAGGIE   But you know that's not true.

ANGELA   Better go and find out.

MAGGIE   Under the dusk dark cherry trees on Middle Meadow walk, go and climb up the stairs of the old Infirmary, polished new and caged in with des res glass . . .

REBUS   (*paperwork*) Why did no fucker write down
             the name of the property company that
             owned the building site? I'm going to get
             the fucker that killed you Maggie I . . .

MAGGIE   (*cutting him off*) Too late for that John. I'll
             still be dead.

ANGELA   And what about me?

MAGGIE   What about my baby girl, Heather?

*Now we hear the music, MAGGIE'S song. REBUS goes and
takes it off.*

ANGELA   Maggie and Heather, Angela and Siobhan.

MAGGIE   And you.

ANGELA   And ex–detective John Rebus.

MAGGIE   Canny save all of us John.

REBUS   (*quiet*) The fuck I can't.

MAGGIE   It's too late.

REBUS   There's a way through this . . . There must
             be . . .

MAGGIE   There's not.

REBUS   There is. There's a way . . .

ANGELA   Time you were on your way John.

Transition into—

Quartermile penthouse, stairwell/flat

MAGGIE and ANGELA are gone. Laboriously, REBUS climbs up to CAFFERTY's penthouse and rings the bell. CAFFERTY lets him in.

CAFFERTY   What's wrong with the lift?

REBUS   Someone's getting a Waitrose delivery.

CAFFERTY   They're supposed to use the service life for that. Come in, come in, take a seat, admire the view. Christ, state of you man. You can have a wee lie down if you like. What are you drinking?

REBUS has semi collapsed.

REBUS   Just give me some water.

CAFFERTY   Bit late to crawl back on the wagon isn't it?

REBUS   *(weary)* Stick some whisky in it then.

CAFFERTY   I've got something better. Going to expand your mind John, wait till you taste this. *(fixing the drink, wine)* This is the best move I ever made, never get tired of that view. You can see half of Edinburgh from up here. 360 degrees of lights and life.

REBUS   And all the world can see you, up here in
             your glass tower.

CAFFERTY   What does that tell you? I'm at the top of
             the world John, nothing to hide, no-one to
             fear now, monarch of all I survey. Is that
             how it goes? I can see you of an evening
             John, down there, having a wee wander in
             the Meadows in the middle of the night.
             Didny know anyone was watching did you?

REBUS   Nothing better on the telly Ger? Thought
             you'd have all the sports channels.

CAFFERTY hands REBUS a glass of wine.

CAFFERTY   Taste that.

REBUS   I'm no a wine drinker.

CAFFERTY   No. No more was I. But try that.

REBUS does so.

CAFFERTY   That's something eh?

REBUS   Is it?

CAFFERTY   Six hundred and fifty pounds a bottle. You
             just sipped twenty quid's worth.

Laughs at REBUS's expression.

CAFFERTY   I know! It's an education John. If you've got that, if you've got the knowledge, you can declare a bottle of second hand plonk is worth a grand or more and no-one will argue with you. That's what it'll be worth.

REBUS   Just get me a water.

CAFFERTY   You're no going to waste that are you? Knowledge. Information. That's always the most valuable commodity there is.

REBUS *is getting his own drink.*

CAFFERTY   Tell you the other thing that makes a wine? Timing. It's worth six hundred today, next year it's tipped over into vinegar. Worthless. But this one is at its best. This is the moment.

REBUS   Why now?

CAFFERTY   The wine?

REBUS   No. Not the wine. Not the fucking wine Cafferty!

CAFFERTY   Not following you.

REBUS   How long have you known I hit you that night?

CAFFERTY   Is that a confession?

REBUS   How long!?

CAFFERTY   From the second I saw those shoes. Twenty-
            five years.

REBUS   And why now? Why are you doing this . . .?

CAFFERTY   *(cutting him off)* What am I doing?

REBUS   Why now!

CAFFERTY   Expert knowledge. You have to know the
            perfect moment, to savour when it's ready.

REBUS   A memory of an ex-squaddies' toe caps? You
            think a jury'll buy that as an identification?

CAFFERTY   Oh I'll say I saw your face on the way down.
            Of course I will, need to make it water
            tight. But the DNA'll back that up eh?

REBUS   You'll lie in the witness box.

CAFFERTY   Of course. Honesty can only get you so far,
            eh John? Sometimes, to get what you want,
            you have to do things your own way. Isn't
            that your philosophy too?

REBUS   You'd let Mordaunt walk free, just so you
            can get me arrested?

CAFFERTY   Will they bother? Sweeping an old has-been
            cop into the bin in his final years? Aye they
            might, you've no made many friends in the
            force, have you John? And you've outlived
            most of those. Yeah they'll probably arrest
            you. That would be a result.

REBUS   What do you want?

CAFFERTY   Nothing. Nothing from you. You're about as much use now as a condom machine on a geriatric ward. My world gets larger every day and yours gets smaller.

SIOBHAN is on, coming to CAFFERTY's door.

CAFFERTY   Sure you won't try more of this wine? I think it just needed to breathe, it's tasting better and better.

SIOBHAN rings the bell. CAFFERTY goes to answer.

CAFFERTY   'Scuse me. Need to get that.

CAFFERTY opens the door.

CAFFERTY   D.I. Clarke. Glad you could make it.

SIOBHAN comes in and stops dead as she sees REBUS.

CAFFERTY   Sorry. Should have told you, you're not the only guest tonight.

SIOBHAN   *(to REBUS)* What are you doing here?

REBUS   You tell me.

CAFFERTY   D.I. Clarke doesn't know a thing. I thought it'd be better if she heard the story from you.

SIOBHAN   What story?

CAFFERTY   Glass of wine D.I. Clarke? White's your poison eh? But I think you'll like this one.

SIOBHAN   What the fuck's going on John?

REBUS   What did he tell you, to get you here?

SIOBHAN doesn't answer, trying to work out what's going on.

REBUS   Siobhan?

CAFFERTY   I told D.I. Clarke I had important information about the defence lawyer's investigation of the attack on me. I told her, if she came here alone, if she could just hold back that impulse to play it by the book, inform her superiors, blah blah . . . If we could just have a private meeting, I'd tell her all about it.

REBUS   And you came? On your own?

CAFFERTY   She learned to bend the rules from the best, eh John.

SIOBHAN   That's what I'm doing here. What about you?

REBUS says nothing.

CAFFERTY   Tell her.

Still nothing.

CAFFERTY   I'm happy to give her my version, just thought you might like to put it in your own words John.

REBUS   I was going to tell you Shiv. It's why I asked you to come with me tonight.

SIOBHAN   Tell me what?

REBUS   Let's go, I'm no talking about it in front of this prick. He's had his fun . . .

CAFFERTY   Christ no! Show's just getting started. I'm the witness for the defence Siobhan. I'm the proof that the police were perfectly prepared to frame Mordaunt back in 1992. I'm the wee hand grenade of truth that's going to blow up twenty-five years of work, trying to put the bastard away. I'll send Mordaunt off singing to a wee retirement home where he'll end his days drinking soup and trying to touch up the carers. But I might not. It depends. There's a deal on the table. Something we should talk about when you know what's going on. Tell her the story Strawman.

REBUS	What deal?! What are you playing at?
CAFFERTY	Tell her now or I tell her.
REBUS	I hit him.
SIOBHAN	What?
REBUS	In 1992. It was me. I hit him across the back of the head with a length of two by two. Wish I'd killed him.
SIOBHAN	But . . . you told me. You *swore* . . . You said none of the officers back then had done any cover up . . .
REBUS	They didn't. It was all me. I'm sorry Siobhan. I am.
SIOBHAN	Tell me. Tell me what happened.
REBUS	*(to CAFFERTY)* Do you remember what you did that night?
CAFFERTY	It's all a blur John, concussion'll do that to a man.
REBUS	We had him. We had him for possession and supply. Five witnesses ready to testify he was the banker, the profiteer, the man making slick money off junky sweat . . . Five witnesses that went to court and magically changed their story under questioning. Even the jury knew they were lying but there was no evidence, every shred of it

threatened and intimidated out of existence
and he sits there, grinning like a toad full
of worms . . .

CAFFERTY   Always the abuse. Enjoy it Strawman,
clock's ticking.

REBUS   He walks out of court. It was the day after
Mordaunt walked out of another court. I
wasn't the lead on Mordaunt or anything
like, but I felt that, like every cop in
Edinburgh. And then Cafferty walks too.

CAFFERTY   *(cutting in)* Oh that was personal eh
Strawman?

REBUS   One wee lassie, we'd spent days coaching
her, reassuring her, promising her we'd
keep her safe . . .

CAFFERTY   He's always promising more than he
delivers. Have you noticed that?

REBUS   She was shaking so hard in the witness
box I thought she'd fall over, and all the
while he's staring at her . . . do you even
remember her Cafferty? Moira Spibey.
Where's she now?

CAFFERTY   Thought it was a police job to keep track of
all the lost souls.

REBUS   Dead. 1996. Overdose.

CAFFERTY   Well, some folk just kill themselves, and
            you canny help them. But have a wee bit
            more of my booze Strawman. If you need it.

REBUS   And this fucker . . . he's just walking about
            a bar . . .

CAFFERTY   My bar. *My* bar Strawman, and why were
            you in there if you weren't looking for me?

REBUS   The night after the trial, grinning, teflon
            coated, all the shite's slid right off him and
            he's grinning like he just ate it all with a
            spoon. Walking about the place, shaking
            hands, patting backs, soaking up the fake
            worship of his dark kingdom of fear . . .

CAFFERTY   Oh fucking poetry now is it? . . . You should
            have seen this one Siobhan, he was barely
            standing, swaying and glowering like a
            drunken prize fighter who doesny know the
            count's finished.

REBUS   He has a word with the barman . . . And
            he's gone. And there's a drink in front of
            me . . .

CAFFERTY   I bought him a drink. And this is what
            happened, because I bought him a drink . . .

REBUS   'Mr Cafferty's compliments, in appreciation
            of all you do to protect the citizens of
            Edinburgh . . .'

CAFFERTY   What was wrong with that?

REBUS   So aye, I followed him into the car park . . .
There's the fucker, no minders for once . . .
He's just standing there, having a smoke.

CAFFERTY   See if I'd only quit sooner in life . . .

REBUS   There's the building timber. Aye. I picked it
up. I swung at him . . . Walked two streets
over. Dumped the two by two. Walked
back. First officer at the scene. And there
it was. Like a last chance. Like a neon
sign flashing 'Get them both John' I saw
Mordaunt's van still parked up in the car
park . . .

CAFFERTY   If I'd only known then how much whisky he
could sink and keep walking . . .

REBUS   And a bar full of witnesses had seen
Mordaunt nip through the back when
Cafferty came in the front.

CAFFERTY   Only way I can figure it is the wee bastard
saw this clown roll up and was feart to get
done for drink driving so he just ran home
and left the van. Ironic, eh?

REBUS   Cafferty went down. Mordaunt went down
for it. Fucking result!

SIOBHAN   What have you done?

REBUS   It was done twenty-five years ago, what do you want?

SIOBHAN   Steve Cant was lack lustre in court? I bet he bloody was! He knew didn't he? The whole squad knew what you'd done . . .

REBUS   Cheering me on.

SIOBHAN   Were they? All of them? Are you sure there weren't more than your boss worried about the day a miscarriage of justice might come back and bite us all? Mordaunt's going to walk John!

REBUS   I'm sorry.

SIOBHAN   What do you want me to tell Angela's father? That you're *sorry*!? Jesus.

CAFFERTY   So. Here's the deal. He was first officer at the scene. He did inspect the evidence once it was located. A little cross contamination, not totally unbelievable eh? Without my sworn evidence of a clear view of his ugly mug it's a bit of mud in the water at worst. I'll withdraw that statement. Concussion, twenty-five years, failing memory, now I think about it I can't be sure, no, I am sure, sure it couldn't have been John Rebus, no, it was a much taller man, thinner, fitter, better looking, nothing like this wreck of an old police officer at all, can't believe I ever

made such a stupid mistake. They won't
even put me on the stand. Probably give
up on the idea of even bringing the assault
evidence into it. Police corruption? No. We'll
just forget about that. Let justice be done.
Let Mordaunt burn. That sound like a good
deal D.I. Clarke?

SIOBHAN   What do you want Cafferty?

CAFFERTY   Just . . . information.

SIOBHAN   What kind of information?

CAFFERTY   Things I need to know. As and when.
The sort of thing a bright D.I. poised for
promotion might happen to be able to pass
on. I'll be no bother at all, the odd phone
call, the odd favour . . .

SIOBHAN   And if I tell you to take a running jump off
your patio there?

CAFFERTY   Mordaunt walks and Rebus is up on
charges of perverting justice and assault.
So. Time to decide what's most important to
you Shiv.

SIOBHAN   Don't call me that!

REBUS *is on the move.*

REBUS   *(to SIOBHAN)* Come on. We're out of here.

SIOBHAN	No . . .
REBUS	Tell him to fuck off and let's get out of here. What? You're seriously thinking about this!?
SIOBHAN	*(quiet)* I have to . . . don't I?
REBUS	No. No. Not happening. You're not going to be his puppet. You're not going to jump when he pulls your strings . . .
SIOBHAN	Mordaunt's going to walk free because you . . . ! *(she can't go on)* Don't talk to me John. Don't even . . . *(she can't speak for another moment. To CAFFERTY)* Can I have a moment? I need to think.
CAFFERTY	You can have a moment. No more.
REBUS	What the fuck is there to think about! Tell him to do his worst! It doesny matter what happens to me now!
SIOBHAN	And what happens to justice for Angela?! What happens to twenty-five years of work and hope and trying . . . I don't give a fuck what happens to you now John. I seriously don't give a fuck! *(to CAFFERTY)* I'm going outside. I'm going to walk round the Meadows. I'll come back.
CAFFERTY	Twenty minutes then. Don't go wandering off.

SIOBHAN   I won't.

She's leaving.

REBUS   I'll come with you.

SIOBHAN   You'll leave me alone!

She's gone.

REBUS looks at CAFFERTY.

CAFFERTY   That was worth waiting for. That was
            almost as good as I ever imagined.

REBUS moves.

CAFFERTY   Don't even try Strawman. There's not
            enough breath left in you to hurt me.

*REBUS hurls the bottle of wine at him. CAFFERTY lets it fly
past.*

CAFFERTY   Fuck it. I'd rather drink vodka anyway.

REBUS has no attack left. Cafferty is getting a drink.

CAFFERTY   Twenty-five years. Fucking flown by eh?
            You and me, head to head, think we've
            finally got a winner eh? Sweet, but kind

of an easy win in the end. Not a contest of equals, but it's been years since you could really give me a fight, eh Strawman? You let yourself go. No the will power to lay off the fags and booze. No the backbone to keep yourself in shape. It's a basic thing see? Staying fit, staying ready. Bottom fucking line. There are still places in the world right now, hunners of them, where staying at the top means keeping the power to batter another man to pulp. The first time you do it, it's terrifying, but after that, well you realise you're just doing what the whole world does to get rich, only difference is you're doing it with your own hands. History. Look at history. The guys with power were the ones who could win a battle with a fucking four-foot blade. I'd've been a king. Bottom. Line. Aye well, no those days is it? Need to move with the times. I'm a dancer Rebus. I've got the fucking moves. You've no even got the music. Shall we put on some music? While we're waiting?

REBUS   If you put on Sheena Easton I'm going over that balcony rail and I'm taking you with me.

CAFFERTY   Stop blackening that woman's name. Just 'cause you canny appreciate proper music.

REBUS   Christ you're a real fan.

CAFFERTY   Always. Named my company after her. One
            of my companies. One of the many many
            wee cubby holes for cash you've never
            found yet John. Pick some music. I've got
            anything you like. Pick a soundtrack for
            your mood.

REBUS   You won't have it.

CAFFERTY   I've got everything.

REBUS   You won't have this.

CAFFERTY   Do you even know what Spotify is you
            fucking dinosaur?

REBUS   Frampton, 'Lines on My Face'.

CAFFERTY is typing it into his phone. Music starts.

CAFFERTY   Straight through the surround system.
            All state of the art. Automatic recording
            of any noise in here too, just in case you
            were hoping there'd be no record of that
            conversation we just had. Fucking digital eh?
            Things you can do. And you lot still struggle
            away with audio tapes like it's 1976.

REBUS   We use audio tapes because you can't doctor
            an audio tape without leaving a trace.

CAFFERTY   It's you that's been leaving traces though.
            Eh John? (*the music*) What the fuck's this
            shite?

He stabs at his phone, fast forwarding.

REBUS   Leave it!

CAFFERTY   A last request? Go on then. You want a soundtrack for defeat? I'll indulge you.

He starts the track again, closer to the end of the song.

CAFFERTY   Winners and losers. What it all comes down to. See, when I was a young man, fighting my way up, this was the prize, the view from the top of Edinburgh. Wankers born to their green acres or banking millions can walk into this. The likes of you and me, we need to fight for it, inch by bloody inch.

REBUS   Aye, you're a social revolutionary Cafferty.

CAFFERTY   But see when a man like me gets it? Gets it all? Fucking unstoppable. 'Cause I've got the millions and I can look any of those soft bastards in the eye and let them see I could punch right through them and it wouldny bother me. I'm terrifying Rebus. I'm ancient power. The original stuff.

REBUS   Original shite.

CAFFERTY   Aw change the record Strawman. We're done. You're finished. Admit it.

REBUS   And you really think, the whole purpose
            of my life was fighting you? Strictly
            supporting cast. Struggle to remember you
            most days.

CAFFERTY   Aye you've a wheen o' regrets right enough
            but no getting me behind bars was the big
            one. Fucking ironic if I put you there. But
            I'd rather have your girl on my keyring.
            That'll be the real victory, the one that'll
            sting you the most.

REBUS   She'll finish you in five seconds if you call
            her a girl to her face.

CAFFERTY   We'll see.

The music's changed to the next track. It is HEATHER's song 'Show Me the Way'.

REBUS   You can turn that up.

CAFFERTY   Turn it off more like. Hate that one.

REBUS   You know it?

CAFFERTY names it.

REBUS   How do you know that one?

CAFFERTY   I'm a complicated man Rebus. You never
            gave me credit for that.

CAFFERTY has stopped the music.

REBUS   You want another track? 'Sympathy for the Devil'?

CAFFERTY   Tell me. Admit it, is there anything I could have done to you that would have hurt you worse than this? Turning Siobhan Clarke against you? Making her my snitch?

REBUS   We don't know what she's going to decide.

CAFFERTY   Aye we do. She won't see Mordaunt walk. And she won't see you go down.

REBUS   No. You hit the bullseye. You win. Only thing worse would be if you'd gone after my daughter.

CAFFERTY   Aye well, I wouldny do that.

REBUS   You'll bring the smell of blood to my doorstep though. Careless. They'll get you for that Cafferty.

CAFFERTY   What are we on about now?

REBUS   The boy, up the stairs from me?

CAFFERTY   Now *that* was a piece of pure cheek. If they knew I was in the building it was.

REBUS   That wasny you?

CAFFERTY   No it wasny me! Fucking amateurs. Come on John. Give me some credit.

REBUS   So who was it?

CAFFERTY   What do you care?

REBUS   There's a girl I need to find. She's in
               trouble.

CAFFERTY   Then she's likely another lost wee thing
               John Rebus can't save.

REBUS seems to slump.

CAFFERTY   *(sings, mocking)* 'Regrets, I've had a few'.
               More than a few eh John?

No answer.

CAFFERTY   How is your daughter by the way? See,
               you've still got something as well as that
               sack of regrets. You've still got her.

REBUS   Biggest regret of the lot. All the ways I've
               failed her.

CAFFERTY   I've no regrets at all. None. Seriously.
               Except maybe that. No kids. A waster son
               that died and didny know me . . .

REBUS   No-one to inherit the royal house of
               Cafferty.

CAFFERTY   No.

REBUS   Nothing makes you vulnerable like a
          child does. Maybe that's the secret of your
          success. They could never really get to you.

CAFFERTY   Maybe. We're drinking now eh?

REBUS   Aye.

CAFFERTY   Good.

Gets them both another.

CAFFERTY   You nearly got me Strawman, I can say it
          now. I did have to scramble to stay ahead of
          you a few times.

REBUS   Good.

CAFFERTY toasts him.

CAFFERTY   To a fucking good fight and the best man won.

REBUS   Who says it's over?

CAFFERTY   Ah come on. Maybe I could adopt. What do
          you think?

REBUS   I'm no sure you'd match the adoption
          agency profile of the ideal parent.

CAFFERTY   Buy a Chinese one. Na. Fuck that. Needs to
          look like me.

REBUS   Sam doesny look much like me.

CAFFERTY   Sure she's yours?

REBUS   Fuck you.

CAFFERTY   She'll have her mother's looks. Way it goes
            eh? DNA. All the mysteries it solves, 'cause
            you canny tell by looking can you?

REBUS   So maybe there's a few monster mini
            Cafferties running around like the wee
            bastards they are.

CAFFERTY   I'd know.

REBUS   But . . .

CAFFERTY   I'd fucking know!

REBUS   Christ. Sore point?

CAFFERTY   Ach. Alright, since we're talking. You never
            got me put away for the heroin dealing you
            said I was doing.

REBUS   That you were doing.

CAFFERTY   That you never caught anyone for doing.
            And how many junkie deaths are we
            talking about?

REBUS   Conscience troubling you?

CAFFERTY   No. Not one bit. But yours is eh? Every
            death another reason to sook on your wee
            bottle. All those poor dead junkie wasters,
            and then there's all the friends and

colleagues, all drowned in the endless sea of John Rebus's mistakes. Your fault. Every one. That's what you think, eh Strawman, that's what you see in the 3 a.m. dark. Regrets. Me? If I've killed anyone . . .

REBUS   *If*!?

CAFFERTY   Casualties of war, every one. Victims of the battle they brought to me. I sleep like a well-fed bairn. Only kind of death I'd ever regret . . . the kind that didn't have to happen. That's why I'd never drink like you. Responsibility of power. You can never lose control. Too dangerous.

REBUS   Sounds like maybe you did then? Just the once.

CAFFERTY   You make mistakes and you learn.

REBUS   What mistakes?

CAFFERTY   One woman. But I learned. Taught me how to behave. You've got another woman on the go I hear. Fuck did you pull that off? How'd you find yet another head case who hates herself so much she'll lie down under a man that regurgitates his own lungs every time he coughs?

REBUS   Trick is to let them go on top.

CAFFERTY   Trick is to buy the best you can afford,
            someone smart enough no even to need to
            fake admiration for the size of your wallet.
            Big money buys you *real* respect from an
            intelligent woman.

REBUS   Aye dream on.

CAFFERTY   It's a weird power relationship you see, men
            and women. If we've got the physical power
            what does that leave them with? Emotional
            manipulation. Fucking dangerous weapon to
            turn on a powerful man, do you not think?

REBUS   You don't like that?

CAFFERTY   Do you?

REBUS   So what're you saying?

CAFFERTY   Nothing. Just there's very little I regret.

REBUS   Except beating up on 'manipulative'
            women?

CAFFERTY   Come on. Worst I've ever done is hand out a
            wee slap to some lassie too cheeky to take a
            telling.

REBUS   Christ you're a feminist icon Big Ger.

CAFFERTY   *(looking at his watch)* She better be back soon.
            Want to text her Rebus?

REBUS   I tell you, I would like to hear that song
            again.

CAFFERTY   No.

REBUS   Bad memories?

CAFFERTY   What?

REBUS   Why do you hate it? Has it got anything to do with a woman. One particular woman?

CAFFERTY   Still the fucking detective.

REBUS   Your only regret?

CAFFERTY   Right. We're done talking about this. Time's up. I'm calling D.I. Clarke back.

REBUS   Easton property development. Not Weston. Something that begins with an 'E'. That the name of your company? Easton property?

CAFFERTY   What about it?

REBUS   You built all those big flats down in Newhaven then.

CAFFERTY   Some of them. That company's sold now. You'll not get anything digging in that mud. My name wasny ever near the paperwork anyway.

REBUS   No you'd have been a bit scary sitting in your best suit eyeballing the ladies and gents of the planning application committee. I heard you were a bit scary altogether, no-one wants to talk about it even now.

CAFFERTY   Talk about what?

REBUS   Maggie Towler.

    A beat.

CAFFERTY   What?

REBUS   Thought she could take on the world . . . Till
            she took on a man she couldny handle.

CAFFERTY   Not following, Strawman.

REBUS   Aye you are. *(sees he's got him)* You are eh?

    He snatches up CAFFERTY*'S phone, keying up the music.*

CAFFERTY   Give me that.

REBUS   How have you even heard of this one?

    'Show Me the Way' is playing again.

CAFFERTY   Switch that off!

    REBUS *is turning up the volume.*

REBUS   Maggie Towler's favourite song. Was it 'your
            tune' Big Ger? Did you wander along the
            the Granton seafront to this one, swinging
            your hands and plotting which foundations
            to drop the bodies in . . .

CAFFERTY   *(snatching for phone, REBUS evading)* Give it!

REBUS   But she'd no have liked all that carry on
eh? Is that what happened? She got a wee
fright when she saw plain what kind of
murdering scum she was shagging? Maybe
she had the idea of letting a few other
people know about the mess she was in?
The police mebbe?

CAFFERTY has got the phone. He cuts the music, breathing heavily.

CAFFERTY   I had nothing to do with Maggie Towler
after 1999. A year or more before she got
herself killed.

REBUS   Interesting turn of phrase.

CAFFERTY   Wasn't even questioned about her.

REBUS   That was careless of someone. Right enough
though, I bet precious few folk knew about
that wee romance. Not your usual type was
she?

CAFFERTY says nothing.

REBUS   Leaving her taste in men aside I heard she
was a nice enough lassie?

CAFFERTY   She was a lying wee hoor.

REBUS   Didn't see her after 1999 you say?

Nothing from CAFFERTY.

REBUS   About the time she fell pregnant?

CAFFERTY   I'm ringing Clarke. I've given her long enough.

REBUS   So all that regret about the Cafferty legacy? A pile of keech eh? You left her high and dry didn't you? Kicked her to the side and never looked back . . .

CAFFERTY   I'd've looked after her!

REBUS   So why didn't you?

CAFFERTY   Bairn wasn't mine. Alright?

REBUS   When did you find that out?

CAFFERTY   Doesny matter . . .

REBUS   Aye it does. Last night she was seen she ducked home early. Way I heard it she saw someone she didn't expect to and it scared her. You had eyes and ears everywhere didn't you, even then.

CAFFERTY   Give it up Strawman. We're no talking about this.

REBUS   You caught her taking the back way home didn't you?

CAFFERTY   I never knew she was pregnant, alright?

REBUS   Canny always be shooting blanks Ger.

CAFFERTY   The bairn was not mine!

REBUS   Is that what she told you? Is that what
            she said? To your face? You wouldny have
            liked that would you? So you get the news,
            she's back on the town, first night out after
            having the kid . . . I bet that was the first
            you knew of the kid eh?

CAFFERTY   You sound like a fucking women's
            magazine, you know that?

REBUS   You catch her going home alone, you ask
            her what she's playing at? Keeping your
            daughter from you . . .

CAFFERTY   Chattering on like a cleaning wifie . . .

REBUS   She says, 'Fuck you, fuck you Big Ger, think
            I'd ever have settled for the limp cxcuse for
            a cock you've got?'

CAFFERTY   Oh you better zip it *right* now!

REBUS   *(cutting over him)* 'Fuck you, I was never with
            you even when you thought I was. Fuck
            you, it's no even your kid!'

*CAFFERTY lays him out. Walks away. Breathing hard. REBUS
picks himself up. Recovers.*

REBUS   And that's what you did. Well no, nothing
            like that. You choked the life out of her eh?
            With her own scarf.

CAFFERTY   What do you think's going to happen now
            Strawman? Think I'm going to break down
            and confess?

REBUS   No need for that. DNA evidence will put
            you in the frame. No doubt.

CAFFERTY   Fuck you talking about?

REBUS   Canny twist a piece of cloth that tight
            without losing a wee bit of skin. Teeny tiny
            bits of Cafferty dust. They couldny get a
            DNA identification at the time, science
            wasny good enough. It is now. Good thing
            they kept the evidence safe eh?

        A beat.

CAFFERTY   Aye right.

REBUS   They really did Big Ger. We checked.
            Yesterday. I was thinking of reopening the
            case.

CAFFERTY   You're no even a policeman. Who's going to
            listen to you?

REBUS   You think I couldny get that done? I knew
            she looked familiar. Should have guessed,

right then. Take away the ugly and I can
see her, right there, on your face . . .

*SIOBHAN is climbing back up, she comes in. CAFFERTY is
just frozen.*

SIOBHAN   Alright. Here's what's going to happen . . .

REBUS   *(cutting her off)* Cafferty's changed his mind.
The deal's off.

SIOBHAN   What?

CAFFERTY'S still frozen.

REBUS   We had a wee talk. He's had a change of
heart.

SIOBHAN   Cafferty?

CAFFERTY   What?

SIOBHAN   The deal's off?

REBUS   He's no longer a witness for the defence.
He's withdrawing his statement. He's
denying he saw any bit of the bastard that
mugged him.

CAFFERTY still doesn't speak.

SIOBHAN   What's going on?

REBUS   A Cold War. Mutually assured destruction.
               It's a 60's thing Shiv. Before your time.

SIOBHAN   *(to CAFFERTY)* Is that right? I need to hear
               you say it.

CAFFERTY   Get him out of here.

SIOBHAN   Are you withdrawing your statement?

CAFFERTY   YES! Now get him out of here before I . . .
               Just get out.

*They start to leave. SIOBHAN is out and on the stair,
recovering. She can't hear the following dialogue.*

CAFFERTY   John . . .

REBUS stops.

CAFFERTY   What do you mean . . . you recognised her?

REBUS   People can say anything Big Ger. Especially
               when they want to get rid of you. Maggie
               lied to you. But DNA canny lie.

CAFFERTY   Where is she? Where's my daughter?

REBUS   I wouldny tell you if I knew.

Transition into—

Stairwell, Quartermile

*SIOBHAN and REBUS on the stair. We see the stairwell but if
the penthouse remains visible CAFFERTY does not move.*

REBUS   Panic over. See? I told you. You just had to
            trust me. It's fixed. I fixed it.

SIOBHAN   Do you know where I've just been, in the
            dark?

REBUS   Round the Meadows?

SIOBHAN   Don't talk to me.

REBUS   Hey. You've seen me bend the rules before.
            You've helped me a few times.

SIOBHAN   The price of losing was never this high.

REBUS   We didn't lose. We won.

SIOBHAN   Yes. I suppose you did.

She's gone into darkness. ANGELA is in front of him.

ANGELA   But I'm still dead.

MAGGIE is there.

MAGGIE   And I'm still waiting.

ANGELA   Nothing solves murder. The dead stay dead.

MAGGIE	You promised me justice. You *promised*!
ANGELA	We're lost in the dark.
MAGGIE	Always.

We see MORDAUNT. *He walks forward.* MAGGIE *and* ANGELA *watch.*

Outside court

SIOBHAN is making a press statement. We still see
MORDAUNT.

SIOBHAN   I have a statement from Angela's father
which I'll read to you now. *(takes it out, reads)*
'Peter Mordaunt has been found guilty and
today our daughter has finally received the
justice she deserves. Nothing can fill the
dark hole she has left in the lives of those
who loved her. Nothing can replace her
spirit or compensate for its loss, but there is
some comfort in knowing that her killer has
finally been identified and punished. All her
surviving family would like to thank the
police for their persistence and dedication
over twenty-five years.'

Lights are going down on MORDAUNT. ANGELA fades away.
MAGGIE is still with REBUS, watching.

SIOBHAN   In return I'd like to thank Angela's family
for their faith in the police over those
twenty-five years. A conviction like the
one we saw today would not have been
possible in 1992. It is possible today
because of advances in science, modern
police techniques. It was not the work of

one but of many, a team, working together
to painstakingly preserve and examine
evidence. No one person could have won
justice for Angela. Good police work is team
work and I'm grateful to each and every
person who built this case. Thank you.

*A flash of press cameras. SIOBHAN is moving away as we
still see REBUS and MAGGIE.*

MAGGIE   What about me?

REBUS   *(quiet)* I'm sorry. I'm sorry Maggie.

MAGGIE   What good's that to me? You let me down
            John.

MAGGIE is gone. REBUS steps into—

Stairwell, Police H.Q.

SIOBHAN is coming downstairs. REBUS is waiting for her.

REBUS   I owe you breakfast.

SIOBHAN says nothing.

REBUS   Saw you on the box. Good stuff. You're
         taking the promotion then? Sounded like a
         Chief Inspector to me.

SIOBHAN What do you want John?

REBUS   Just . . . wanted to say congratulations. You
         got him.

SIOBHAN Yes. We got him.

REBUS   Well done.

SIOBHAN Thanks.

REBUS   Got to be worth a cappuccino, come on . . .

SIOBHAN What have you got on Cafferty?

A beat.

REBUS   I can't tell you that Shiv.

Another beat. Then SIOBHAN'S moving.

SIOBHAN   'Course not.

REBUS   Siobhan . . .

SIOBHAN   (cutting him off) But it's something big,
           something that could put him away for
           good, something that scares him. And the
           thing is John, the thing I've worked out is,
           that if we didn't have to keep him quiet
           about your drunken, stupid violence, we
           could turn that weapon on Big Ger. We
           could use it. We could put him away. But
           hey, Mordaunt's finally locked up eh? That
           what they called a win? In your day?

           SIOBHAN is gone. REBUS waits a moment then moves into—

Stairwell, Arden Street

Slowly REBUS *starts to walk up the stairs.* HEATHER *is sitting on the stairs.*

REBUS   Where did you go to?

HEATHER   Och . . . around and about. You know.

REBUS *is taking his phone out.*

REBUS   I need to call this in . . .

HEATHER   *(urgent)* Don't! Wait till I'm gone. I just wanted to know if you'd found anything. About my Mum.

A beat..

HEATHER   It's lost history isn't it? Didn't realise I was hopeful but . . . That's stupid eh? The way you can keep hoping. Like still believing in Santa . . . or life after death. Look it's ok. As long as you tried.

REBUS   You have to talk to the police, Heather, about the night Andy was killed.

HEATHER   No!

REBUS   Why not?

HEATHER   Don't call them.

REBUS   Well I have to . . .

He stops as HEATHER *takes out a gun and points it at him.*

HEATHER   Stupid fucker didn't think I'd use a knife
            so he came at me. That's when I knew I
            needed a gun. Should have realised: if you
            don't look like you're big enough to give
            them a doing they will try eh? And that's
            just messy. And upsetting. I need folk to
            stand still when I'm talking to them.

REBUS   Right.

HEATHER   If I'd had a gun that night I probably
            wouldny have had to use it. But he thought
            he could take me. Stupid fuck.

REBUS   You were supplying Andy. You were his
            boss.

HEATHER   And he was a fucking idiot. All he had to do
            was take the business off the stair. Like you
            said. You noticed. You knew exactly what he
            was doing. Can't have folk working for me
            that are that kind of stupid. I wouldny have
            killed him but . . . Like I said, he tried to
            take me. *(breaks off)* What are you looking at
            me like that for?

REBUS   That's the business plan is it Heather? This is how you're going to make your fortune?

HEATHER This is just how I'll get started. Then I'll diversify.

REBUS   Thing is, when you've got a toe in one world, it's awfy hard to pull it loose and jump into another.

HEATHER Richard Branson kick started his millions by fiddling his VAT.

REBUS   Is that a fact? Och you'll be fine then.

HEATHER All I'm doing is what the whole world does to get rich.

REBUS   Only difference is you're doing it with your own hands.

HEATHER That's right.

REBUS   Must be in your blood.

HEATHER What do you mean?

REBUS   Remember your mum Heather. She'd want you to do that.

HEATHER Sometimes I kid on she's watching me. Think she'd be proud John?

REBUS   I think she'd be worried for you. There's sharks out there Heather. Seriously sharp teeth.

HEATHER   I can look after myself. Better than she
           could. Maybe I take after my Dad eh? What
           do you think?

REBUS   Careful what you wish for.

HEATHER's on the move.

HEATHER   You can make your phone call now. I'm
           going. See you around John.

She's leaving.

REBUS   I won't do that. I won't call it in.

HEATHER   *(stopped)* Why not?

REBUS   *(offering her a card)* Because one day, if you
           ever meet the biggest shark out there, you
           should phone me.

HEATHER   Why?

REBUS   Because if you meet him, you'll really need
           my help.

HEATHER   And what's in it for you?

REBUS   Maybe something we called a win . . . back
           in my day.

HEATHER   Alright. I'll do that.

She takes the card and leaves. After a moment REBUS
follows her down the stairs. The song, HEATHER *and*
MAGGIE'S *song starts and swells in volume.*

We see CAFFERTY *lit up in his penthouse, staring out over
the city.*

REBUS *is in the Meadows, staring up towards* CAFFERTY'S
*penthouse. They can't see each other but each knows the
other is there.*

Music hits a crescendo.

BLACKOUT.

IAN RANKIN and RONA MUNRO

In conversation

Ian: So, Rona, what were your feelings when you were first approached about *Long Shadows*?

Rona: My first reaction was that I hadn't read the books with enough attention! I think my brain clicked into 'homework' mode. Years of encounters with John Rebus, purely for pleasure, didn't seem to qualify me for the responsibility. Of course, I then re-read the novels, especially the ones that focused on that strange, potent dynamic between Rebus and Cafferty. That reminded me that reading for pleasure was the point; that's why the books are so fantastic. The job was to try and transfer that appreciation to the stage in a way that was theatrical but also satisfying to fans of the books.

Ian: Yes, I was certainly keen to see your 'take' on that powerful relationship between Rebus and Cafferty. The two share an empathy but also an antipathy. They seem to me like warring sides of the same split personality – and as you know I've always had a fascination for books such as R L Stevenson's *Dr Jekyll and Mr Hyde* and James Hogg's *Memoirs and Confessions of a Justified Sinner*. I was also interested in the way you had dealt with masculine/royal power (and disempowerment) in your *James Plays* for the National Theatre of Scotland. Scotland is such a small country, I think people outside reckon all the writers must know each other, but we had somehow conspired never to bump into one another until we started bouncing ideas around about a Rebus stage play. Do you remember the early stages of that working relationship?

Rona: Well, I think we made it up as we went along, didn't we? I don't know about you, but I always felt that it had to be as organic as a conversation. I didn't go into the project with any expectations of how we would work together. I thought we'd probably just start from that first mug of coffee and chocolate biscuit in your living-room and see what felt comfortable. I think every creative collaboration I've ever been part of has depended on mutual respect and trust. In this case, the biggest leap of trust probably came from you – Rebus is yours, after all. I know you've let others get their sticky paws on him with TV adaptations, and you seem very laid back and not at all possessive of the great man. Is that something you've had to work at or did you always feel able to detach?

Ian: I think it was easier to detach in the early years. When the first Rebus novel came out, there was immediate TV interest from Leslie Grantham (who was famous at the time for playing Dirty Den on BBC's *East Enders*). He wanted to move the action to London so he could play Rebus as a London cop. I took one look at the fee being offered and I was delighted with that. But then it never happened. I think throughout my years with Rebus I've come to accept that he belongs to everybody, most notably his fans. You and I did discuss this, I remember – we wanted to produce a play that would engage lifelong fans while still being accessible to an audience who might not know the books but love a night out at the theatre. I know you hadn't worked with the whodunit genre previously – did the format present you with particular issues as a playwright?

Rona: I think it depends on the whodunit, doesn't it? Drama is always a *why*dunit – that's what creates drama, the emotions and character backstories are what creates the action. A whodunit then needs a twist which satisfies, a plot twist, something the audience can't see coming but which satisfies when it does. There are very skilfully created detective novels that provide a puzzle or a plot twist but don't necessarily have character change. I don't think that kind of story transfers well to the theatre stage. Fortunately, the Rebus novels have always been as much about character – and character development – as plot. Over the course of the series we've been able to watch Rebus shift his views as he ages and takes in the moral lessons of the various cases he has worked on.

Ian: Yes, I think from the get-go we both felt this had to work both as a twisty psychological thriller and as a study in character. What did you feel the stage version of Rebus could bring out that the novels couldn't?

Rona: You get to see the characters live in real-time. I think that has an excitement – as all theatre does – that's unique. The characters appear in living, breathing 3D in front of the audience.

Ian: Yes, when I go to the theatre I feel a level of participation in these characters' lives that rarely happens when they are on a screen, big or small. But let's go back to the process, because as well as working with me, you were also liaising with the play's director – can you say a little about that?

Rona: Where do I start? The relationship between playwright and director is a particularly close one in theatre. In this case, of course, it's essentially a relationship between *two* writers and a director, and I think with new writing the director is an essential conduit between the writer's intentions and the actors' portrayal of those intentions. A good director understands what you meant by any particular line of dialogue and what's working about the drama. They then know how to translate that into instructions and support that the actors will find useful or vital. Directors can also let you know when your intentions – what those lines of dialogue *need* to convey – is not surviving the test of the rehearsal room.

Ian: Not so dissimilar from the relationship between novelist and editor. A good editor makes the book better by pointing to where lines, scenes or characters don't work or could work better.

Rona: Yes, sometimes what's in the playwright's head needs a rewrite to make it into better theatre. I always sit in on the first part of the rehearsal process and fully expect to have to 'tweak' a script (at the very least!) once we get things up on their feet and being played out live in that room.

Ian: God, I remember that experience from *Dark Road*. As a novelist, once the book is printed and bound, you can't make any more alterations or improvements – you're stuck with it. But right up until the previews, with a paying audience seeing that play for the first time, cuts and tweaks were being made. I remember one whole scene being cut by the director (who also happened to be the co-writer) and I thought: really? You can do that? The actors don't mutiny? But those edits are always there for a purpose – to make the play as cohesive, coherent, and satisfying as possible. Of course, I was aware that you had worked with Roxana before and you really rated her, so that made the whole relationship easier. I recall the three of us enjoying more coffee and biscuits in my living-room, and the occasional brainstorming session over a meal.

Rona: We were challenged weren't we? Our plot was interrogated with steely determination and we had to find the answers to a lot of probing questions! But I think the story became better for it.

Ian: Of course, we were writing a new Rebus adventure from scratch rather than adapting one of the existing stories. Do you recall how that decision was made? And is it easier than trying to adapt?

Rona: I can answer the second part of that but not the first. As a playwright I think adapting a novel for the stage is straightforward, insofar as the majority of plot- and character-decisions have already been taken for you. However, it is problematic when the form of the narrative needs a lot of wrestling to fit into an evening's theatre. A very long novel with multiple scenes and flashbacks would, for example, present particular difficulties. I think a meaty short story is actually probably a much easier fit. But to bounce that back to you, why did you decide that we two should concoct a story between us and develop it collaboratively rather than present me with a completed narrative (in short story form, say)?

Ian: Ach, I think I just wanted to hang out with a great contemporary playwright and watch how their mind works, maybe learning some new skills or at least stretching myself along the way. Creative writers are very different in their attitudes, working methods and ways of seeing (and then presenting) the world. The relationship between Rebus and Cafferty is very male working-class, very macho, very Scottish. I wanted to watch how you would approach that. Our lengthy discussions made me think deeply about my own understanding (or lack of it) of these two characters – not forgetting Siobhan Clarke, who also has an important role to play in *Long Shadows*! As a novelist, of course, I have the lazy privilege of being able to use as many scenes, locations, words and characters as I like. Did you find any problem with retaining the atmosphere of the books within the necessary restrictions of a stage play?

Rona: Well, that was made easier because we did develop the story from scratch rather than try to shoehorn in some pre-existing narrative. It was a lot easier to concentrate the action in time and space. I also feel that a lot of the 'action' in your books is actually internal – it is formed of Rebus's observations of and reactions to events. That's a good fit for the stage as it can be shown in ways that are very theatrical.

Ian: I certainly enjoyed the journey, Rona.

Rona: Me, too. See you in the theatre!

ROXANA SILBERT, BIRMINGHAM REPERTORY THEATRE'S ARTISTIC DIRECTOR

On bringing Rebus to the stage

Were you very aware that this is the first time onstage for a character who's existed in other mediums, especially books but also more than one TV adaptation, as well as radio? Was that something that was on your mind?

We were really aware, because Ian has been approached quite often, either to adapt his work or to allow his work to be adapted, or to write something for the theatre. And obviously you're dealing with a very iconic character, who readers absolutely adore. And that part of it is daunting, because you feel you have a real responsibility to not let them down.

How did that impact on your approach?

What mostly happens with things like novel adaptations is that there is a novel that a playwright adapts for the stage. And so, it is an adaptation of a story that already exists. What's unique about this is that Ian has written a new story for the stage, alongside a playwright. So, it's not that Rona Munro adapted this story, it's that Ian has written it, and then they've worked very closely together to create the play.

As a result, when sometimes there might be something in the writer's head that's not really hitting the page – you often ask those questions of a playwright – in this case, I could ask those questions directly of Ian, who knows those people inside out. So even if something wasn't clear on the page, it was absolutely vivid in his imagination, and then he was able to describe it in such a way that Rona could make it work for the stage. Novel writing and playwrighting are so different. I always think novels are more like film, in the sense that you can get inside someone's head and you can work out what they're thinking, and you don't have to have a lot of action because you can have a lot of internal monologue. But, with theatre you only really know people by what they say and what they do, and so it's a much more behavioural writing mode. Adaptations are always very challenging for that reason. So, doing it this way seemed to me the best of both worlds.

Because Rebus is a detective character and the books are crime novels, did you think much about the genre, more than in other plays?

In this particular instance, we thought about it a lot as a thriller. Rona is an avid thriller reader. She knew the Rebus books inside out before she was ever approached to work on them. One of the things we talked about a lot was that Rebus is a detective, so there has to be a crime to be solved. Looking at the evolution of the script, we have been very aware that it's a detective story. What Ian and Rona have written into this, is that Rebus is a character who has a lot of demons, and those live in his head. One of the things theatre can do is make those manifest, and physicalise them and make them 3-D. So that's one of the things that theatre has allowed him to do.

I think the other thing that Rona's done brilliantly is writing a series of really strong and long dialogues. Interestingly, that's not something you can do on film or in novel writing. In film, you have lots of short scenes, you can't really sit in a dialogue for twenty minutes. It is a particularly theatrical thing you can do, which has allowed us to stay with these characters that we know really well, like Rebus and Cafferty and Siobhan, and watch the minutiae of their interaction over a sustained period of real-life time. So I think that that's coinciding with being absolutely honourable to the form that he writes in, to the character and being a detective story, but also asking why are you going to do this on stage, why aren't you going to do this in a different medium? Because there is Rebus on radio, there is Rebus on television – so why are people going to want to see a play?

We had to think why does this work for the stage and not for the television or a novel? Why is this story better told onstage?' One of the things Ian had said, which I think is really smart, is he hadn't wanted to write something until he felt he had a Rebus story that could only be told on the stage. And that was a really good way in for us understanding the story. For example, the way it's designed is absolutely taking on board the noir thriller genre. It's designed to feel very much like a thriller. A lot of inspirations have come from the noir thriller cinematic feel.

Theatre is a very collaborative medium but if you have the creator of the Rebus character there, did ownership come into it or was it as purely collaborative as theatre usually is?

It's been incredibly collaborative – I have to say that Ian has allowed it to be so, he's been very generous. What is not collaborative is that no one can know those characters better than he knows those characters, but that would be true of any playwright or any primary artist. But in terms of how you turn that story into something that works on stage, he has worked incredibly collaboratively with Rona, and how we, director Robin Lefevre, designer Ti Green and the production team at Birmingham Repertory Theatre, turn what's on the page into something that's going to be onstage.

In reality, what that means is that you're constantly having a dialogue. We sat down and said who are the people you would like to see onstage playing Rebus; who would you like to see playing Siobhan; this is the world as I imagine it. So, it's been really necessarily collaborative and I've learnt – because of course I've read and loved the novels – so much more about Ian's approach to those characters through having access to him which has been fantastic.

Were there any themes particularly that spoke to you? Is that something that's important to you, to approach it on that level or are you led by what's interesting others in the first instance?

It has to strike at your heart – something in you has to be emotionally moved by it. What I found really interesting was the idea that you want to love Rebus for being a maverick and wanting to play outside the rules, but the story also really doesn't romanticise the consequences of being a maverick. Someone is caught and someone goes to prison for a crime that they did, but someone else doesn't and actually there is an inference that if you'd gone by the book and done it the right way – and it would have been a bit laborious and a bit boring and a bit administrative – but actually the result might have been a truer result. I think there's a fascinating tension because it's about how you choose to live your life, and whether you choose to live your life in the system or out of the system and what the pros and cons are. But it's quite a dispassionate look at that. It doesn't really say 'this is the way to do it, we should all be romantic, outside-the-loop kind of people'. Because there are consequences to that, there are hard lessons to learn from it, and you wonder too 'do I always want to be inside the system?'

I also think in this particular story Rebus's relationship to young women – his desire to protect them – the huge cost to these young women of living a life that is slightly on the edges, is of enormous interest to me as well. And there's just something about the world of the detectives or the high calibre criminal that Cafferty is. It's not my world and it's always fascinating. I'm sure it's true of all arts but sometimes what's fascinating about theatre is that it reflects a world, an experience that you're living which it helps you process, but sometimes it's an introduction to a world that you do not live in. Ian's writing is so authentic and his knowledge of that world so profound that you feel you are genuinely glimpsing something that is usually behind closed doors.

Finally, I think because Rebus is now retired, and his way of policing – which is really hands-on, going to the bar where the incident happened and tracking someone down by foot – has been superseded by technology because most police work is now done at computers. Of course, there is a sense of nostalgia but there's also a sense that he's out of touch. The pros and cons, the benefits and risks of the different types of policing – which is a metaphor for a lot of the way the world is going – is again very intriguing. It's also so human because he can't race upstairs like he used to because he's a man in his sixties! His back's not great, and he can't chase or and escape criminals because he's a bit tired. I love that humanity in it, I love that he has become an older man who is retired, who's struggling with technology, and who walks into police stations or places where he would have known everybody and knows nobody because there's a new generation of people there. It's a very interesting, slightly painful, look at late middle-age and how you've shifted and moved on.

And it sort of magnifies the loneliness of being a maverick as well, that he's left with Cafferty as his closest friend and his biggest enemy – I've always found that dynamic between them really fascinating.

Yes, absolutely – the loneliness of deciding to go your own path.

That's the cost, isn't it? And that's why most of us don't and why we respect these heroes on-screen and on-stage who do.

Because it's glamorous in your twenties and thirties. It's less glamorous in your sixties or seventies!

Yes, because you're left with the bill at the end of all that when you've isolated everyone and taken all these turns.

And your family – his daughter is estranged, he doesn't have a partner, his friendships are tenuous, you mentioned Cafferty. It's fascinating.

How much did you want to recreate the atmosphere of Edinburgh onstage? Given that it's such a huge part of the books and on screen – was that a key aspect for you in terms of design and direction?

Edinburgh is another character in those novels. I lived and worked in Edinburgh for five years and met Rona in Edinburgh and our first shows were in Edinburgh – so I have a tremendous emotional connection to Edinburgh, it's a city I really love.

The challenge in the play is that you're in lots of different environments – mainly in Rebus's front room – and so we were looking for a space that would allow us to move fluidly between a pub, to a tower block, to his house. The designer, Ti Green, and I felt that those stairwells – which is the kind of flat that Rebus lives in – are very iconic to Edinburgh and that we wanted something that was really simple and sculptural.

We weren't trying to be naturalistic in our setting, but so that we were able to move between locations while keeping Edinburgh in the forefront, the stairwells became the focus of how we moved forward in the design. We were really lucky because we are working with a Scottish production manager and so he's a very good reality test of what we're doing. And it comes down to things like the paint finish – we can get the shape of the stairwell right but then you have to look at the paint finishes, it's all in those details. If you have a very abstract sculptural space, then every object you put in becomes significant and has to tell a story. So those are the kind of conversations that we had.

Music has always been such a huge part of the novels. How important is music to this script and the production?

One of the things, of course, is that Rebus has very specific musical tastes and music is key in the detective storytelling of the play, so we have a composer who is going to write a new score for the play but also work quite closely with Ian to identify the right kinds of songs for Rebus to listen to. It's just a really important part of Rebus's world, the songs that he listens to. In terms of the questions you asked about genre, obviously music is quite a key part to that – you can tell a lot of story through music – so that's another really strong component of the design and the storytelling.

Do you have a favourite scene or moment in the script that you think most about?

I think what really drew me was the way that those scenes are like a staircase – they lead up to that final confrontation. I read the play like I would read a thriller,

I really wanted to know what happened. That is exciting to me because you need every moment, and it felt like no moment was wasted. And that, I thought, was quite genius.

SET DESIGN BY TI GREEN

Photography (unless otherwise stated): Gil Gillis ARPS

Early white card model of the set design (pub scene)

Early white card model of the set design (forensic lab)

Exploring texture and tone in the model (upper landing and curved staircase)

Exploring texture and tone in the model (whole stage)

Final model (Rebus's apartment and neutral environment).
Credit: Ti Green

Final model (pub). Credit: Ti Green

BIRMINGHAM REPERTORY THEATRE

Birmingham Repertory Theatre Company is one of Britain's leading producing theatre companies. Its mission is to inspire a lifelong love of theatre in the diverse communities of Birmingham and beyond. As well as presenting over sixty productions on its three stages every year, the theatre tours its productions nationally and internationally, showcasing theatre made in Birmingham.

The commissioning and production of new work lies at the core of The REP's programme and over the last fifteen years, the company has produced more than 130 new plays. The theatre's outreach programme engages with over 7,000 young people and adults through its learning and participation programme, equating to 30,000 individual educational sessions. The REP is also committed to nurturing new talent through its youth theatre groups, and training up and coming writers, directors and artists through its REP Foundry initiative. The REP's Furnace programme unites established theatre practitioners with Birmingham's communities to make high quality, unique theatre.

Many of The REP's productions go on to have lives beyond Birmingham. Recent tours include *What Shadows*, *The Government Inspector*, *Of Mice And Men*, *Anita And Me*, *Back Down*, *Nativity! The Musical* and *The King's Speech*. The theatre's long-running production of *The Snowman* celebrates its 25th anniversary in 2018 and also its 21st consecutive Christmas season in the West End.